DEATH AND DECONSTRUCTION

Anne Fleming

Chivers Press • Thorndike Press
Bath, Avon, England   Thorndike, Maine USA

This Large Print edition is published by Chivers Press, England, and by Thorndike Press, USA.

Published in 1996 in the U.K. by arrangement with Robert Hale Limited.

Published in 1996 in the U.S. by arrangement with St. Martin's Press, Inc.

U.K. Hardcover   ISBN 0–7451–4782–8 (Chivers Large Print)
U.K. Softcover   ISBN 0–7451–4790–9 (Camden Large Print)
U.S. Softcover   ISBN 0–7862–0636–5 (General Series Edition)

The right of Anne Fleming to be identified as author of this work has been asserted by her in accordance with the Copyright, Designs and Patents Act 1988.

The text of this Large Print edition is unabridged.
Other aspects of the book may vary from the original edition.

Set in 16 pt. New Times Roman.

Printed in Great Britain on acid-free paper.

British Library Cataloguing in Publication Data available

Library of Congress Cataloging-in-Publication Data

Fleming, Anne.
    Death and deconstruction / Anne Fleming.
      p. cm.
    ISBN 0–7862–0636–5   (lg. print : lsc)
    1. Byron, George Gordon Byron, Baron, 1788–1824—Manuscripts—Fiction.   2. Romanticism—Societies, etc.—Fiction.   3. Poetry—Societies, etc.—Fiction.   4. Large type books. I. Title.
[PR6056.L39D4 1996]
823'.914—dc20   95–47312

AUTHOR'S NOTE

Although the Coleridge and Other Romantic Poets Society shares some characteristics with the Byron Society it is neither the Byron Society, the Keats-Shelley Memorial Association nor any other real society. None of the characters in this book bears any relation to any member of those societies, either living or dead, or to any member of any other society. They are figments of the author's imagination.

Anne Fleming

FOREWORD

I apologize for the liberties I have taken with Norman Abbey, its opening times, its security system, its custodian and keepers and, most of all, for holding an imaginary conference on its premises, placing an imaginary hotel on the site of the old stables and hanging an imaginary copy (much enlarged in size) of Giorgione's *Tempesta* in the Orangery.

I apologize to Nottinghamshire Constabulary for creating an imaginary member of that force.

I apologize to the London Library for adding an imaginary Mr Mablethorpe to their staff.

I apologize to the House of Lords for creating an imaginary member of the peerage, Lord Hellvellyn.

And, finally, I am most grateful to Lord Ralph Kerr for allowing me to use his name so that I need not create an imaginary owner of Melbourne Hall, to Mr John Murray for allowing me to mention his name and his publishing house, to the Wordsworth Trust at Grasmere and to Mr Howard Usher, archivist at Melbourne Hall.

CHAPTER ONE

*Marry, this is miching mallecho; it
means mischief.*

SHAKESPEARE

It was only when it was all over, when they had
been fished out of the water and taken back to
their *pensione* and hotels to prepare for the
evening reception at the Palazzo Mocenigo
that it dawned on the members that someone
had tried to drown the Coleridge and Other
Romantic Poets Society in the Venetian
Lagoon.

It had been a magical afternoon on the
Island of San Lazzaro, poised between sea and
sky, peaceful as the angelus hour, far from the
beat and hum and shrill of the city. As they
prepared to leave the island the Armenian
monks smiled gently on them all—the men in
their blazers and lightweight suits, the women
with their handbags and hairdos, the girls in
their summer frocks and sandals, jeans,
leggings, baggy tops, and the eccentrics in their
cloaks, ethnic robes, drooping cotton sunhats.

There was much shaking of hands and a final
clustering round the tall bearded monk who
had guided them round the monastery, shown
them its treasures, taken them into the chapel
for a service brilliant with candles heavy with

1

incense and spell-binding with chanting from the monks. He had shown them the very room where Byron had come to learn the Armenian language and the place where the poet had sat with the monks in the gardens, looking out across the waters of the Lagoon towards the roofs and towers and domes of Venice, which always seemed from here to be floating insubstantially on her hundred isles.

This was one of the high points of the Byron and Shelley Tour of Italy, which had taken them to castles and villas, great libraries and art collections, all doors open to them (which as private individuals they might never have entered). The academic members were more interested in the conference which had been held at the University of Venice and gave them the chance to foregather with their colleagues from other countries. But many of them enjoyed the frivolities quite as much as their fellow members and were equally delighted at being presented to a princess, an ambassador, an earl or a vice chancellor while pursuing their studies of the Romantic poets.

'Thank you, Father! *Merci, mon père!* Goodbye! *Arriverderci!*' And they clambered down towards the hired motor launches that were to bear them across the windless, flat and shining waters to the Accademia.

It was still hot but the sun was lower in the sky and the light distinctly less dazzling. It took time to usher the party into the boats. The

2

camera enthusiasts kept dashing off to take a last photograph and there was a certain amount of manoeuvring as some tried to seat themselves beside the socially or academically exalted members. Eventually all were embarked and the boatmen cast off.

The last boat to start was slightly delayed. It shot forward then jolted to a stop, its engine stalled. The boatman, who had a flagon of wine concealed beside the wheel, had forgotten to cast off the mooring rope. An ex-naval man quietly stepped ashore, performed this task and stepped on board again. The boatman shrugged his shoulders and saluted gratefully with a shame-faced grin. A high female voice was heard to utter, in tones familiar in the Shires, 'Had he forgotten to untether it, then?' and the boat leaped forward for Venice.

As it caught up with the last of the other boats a loud bang and a flash of fire came from the stern of that boat. It moved forward but, with every foot it gained, the hull descended an inch lower into the water. Someone screamed. The boatman threw up his hands and called on his gods. The passengers were now on their feet. Then they were in the water and the boat which had been so luckily delayed was alongside to come to their aid.

The screams of the members of the society as they were immersed in the water brought their plight to the notice of the other boatmen, now some way ahead. After a moment of incredulity they brought their launches round, each in its own wide arc, and came with all speed to the rescue.

Their late host was even quicker. He stepped down into a fair-sized craft which was used for fetching supplies to the monastery and shot out to pick up a brace of ladies treading water in smart linen coats and skirts and an elderly gentleman in a panama hat doing a feeble breaststroke. With his help soon all the dripping passengers had been fished out of the water and were standing on dry land.

The monks begged them to come into the monastery for brandy and a change of clothing but after some discussion they decided to be taken straight to their hotels. They felt dubious about the monastic plumbing and preferred to arrive at the Pensione Accademia or, in some cases the Danieli or the Gritti, in wet clothes rather than to walk through Venice wrapped in monkish robes. The victims were distributed between the other boats.

So the Coleridge and Other Romantic Poets Society (sometimes known as RPS) set off once again for Venice. The boatless boatman sat in the stern of one of the boats with his head in his hands. As he tenderly handed the ladies ashore at the Accademia he fixed his eye on Martin Proctor, the chairman, and Ninian Wallace, his deputy, the two leaders of what he regarded as a motley collection of madmen and women, and he said, 'It was done on purpose.'

4

'On purpose?'

'You heard the bang. All the boats are in good order. Some beastly villain has put explosive in my boat. Someone has tried to murder the members of your party.'

'Hush!' said Martin authoritatively. But the members were intent on hot baths and brandies and titivation and tea. It had been very alarming; it might have been terrorists, the act of a madman, or perhaps the result of a feud between rival boat firms. In Italy who could tell? But it was safely over.

So far no one had speculated on the possibility that this might be no more than the opening salvo.

CHAPTER TWO

Flat burglary as ever was committed.
                              SHAKESPEARE

Martin Proctor was a man of medium height who looked more like a high-ranking army officer than a literary man although he was a director of Hackett and Hill's Literary Agency. His thick white hair was neatly parted and severely flattened down. His eyes were grey and cold but they grew warm when he was in the company of young people, children and the members of his own family. In appearance he was always trim and subfusc, wearing dark suits and heavy silk ties in the evening and tweeds and brogues and woollen ties by day.

His flat in St John's Wood was as trim and orderly as himself. A few sporting prints, some family portraits, drawings of the Romantic poets and a Lear watercolour of Greece were the only adornments on the walls apart from bookshelves. Vast sash windows looked out on a long and leafy garden. He had no part in either the amenities or the upkeep of this garden but his balcony overlooked it and was hung with jasmine and wisteria.

His books overflowed into a large old-fashioned kitchen where he ate ready-made meals. He was often invited out for dinner and repaid the hospitality of his friends by taking them to pleasant and unusual eating places which were only moderately expensive; a bistro in a quiet street near Ladbroke Grove, a garden restaurant in Stoke Newington, an old-fashioned pub in a mews in Fulham, a wine bar near the river at Kew.

Six years earlier his wife had driven her car on to black ice, skidded into a lamp post, and ended up in hospital in a coma. Four years later she developed pneumonia and died. It was soon after that that he had become chairman of RPS thus making sure that most of his spare time was filled with activities of what he felt to be a moderately useful kind.

Martin Proctor proved an efficient chairman

who dealt sharply with those whose noses had been put out of joint by his election. But his lack of animosity was so evident that he ended by making friends of all of them—friends, however, of a special sort. It was not the friendship of peer with peer but that of an army commander with his staff, affable but aloof. This particularly annoyed Ninian Wallace who had been treasurer of the society for several years and had hoped to become chairman. The deputy chairmanship was consolation but not atonement for this disappointment.

Ninian was a remarkably handsome man, tall, auburn-haired, broad-shouldered and muscular, blue-eyed with sensitive bony features. Like many who possess this degree of beauty he felt that he ought to command some sort of return for it; if not adoration then at least admiration and admittance to the intimacy of the prominent among his circle. When this was not vouchsafed to him he tended to sulk. And he was still sulking mildly over Martin's appointment. He had always devoted more time to the society than Martin and ignored the fact that one reason for this had been the daily visits Martin had made to his wife in hospital.

Ninian's wife was a pale copy of himself, tall, auburn-haired and beautiful but vapid. He had married her for her beauty and was suffering the consequences. They had little in common. She was PA to Matthew Frost of the Frost business empire. Ninian had got her the job through RPS of which Frost was an enthusiastic patron and he was irritated to find that she earned more than he did. She resented the fact that he took it for granted that she should work, and they tended to bicker embarrassingly in public.

When they landed at Heathrow on their way home from the RPS foray to Venice, Martin accepted a lift home from Ninian who had left his battered Ford in the airport car-park. (Lavinia had stayed an extra day in Venice for an art exhibition.)

As they rattled towards St John's Wood, Martin said, 'Now we can talk. Can the bomb really have been meant for us?'

'The Questore thought not.'

'He's probably right. It's much more likely to have been a disgruntled employee or a rival boat firm. But we'll never know for certain. Even if they get the boat up the evidence is hardly likely to have survived.'

'I can't imagine who would play such a trick on RPS.'

'They can't possibly have intended to drown anyone. It must have been a hoax.'

'Pretty ruthless hoaxer and pretty pointless hoax. What could he hope to gain by it?'

'Just to annoy us I suppose. Could one of our lot have sneaked off while we were going round the monastery?'

'I should think nothing could be easier. But

8

he'd presumably have had to get into the water to fix the explosives. He'd have been wet through.'

'No. It would have been in the bilges and set for the blast to go downwards. The Questore said they can do anything at all with explosives nowadays. How could he be sure the blast wouldn't damage the people in the boat? It's an alarming thought, isn't it?'

'I suppose one of our people could have paid someone else to do it but have we anyone dotty enough for that? And he'd probably have had to speak Italian.'

'Well, that includes about a quarter of the party. All the Italians, several of the American academics, you and me and the princes.'

'I think it's all too far-fetched. It must have been a local feud.'

'It would be nice to think so.'

They talked of the success of the seminar at the University of Venice and the plans for the conference at Norman Abbey the following June.

'Come in for a drink,' said Martin as they pulled up outside one of the large houses on Hamilton Terrace.

'I don't think I will, if you don't mind. Better get on home and sort myself out.'

Martin was persistent and, as usual, he got his way. The two men walked upstairs to the third-floor flat, went in, and stopped short, shocked into a sudden stillness.

The door of the drawing-room was open and they could see that the room had been devastated. Bookcases had been overturned, pictures torn down, drawers emptied of their contents, flung on the floor and the filing cabinets upturned on top of them.

Martin's face went dark red and he breathed heavily. He walked slowly round the room examining the wreckage.

'Police,' said Ninian. 'Where's the phone?'

'No,' said Martin, 'no police.'

'No police? But surely—'

'This looks like malice,' said Martin. 'I can't see anything has gone.'

He squatted down to look into an upturned cupboard, stretched up to run a hand along a shelf.

'It's worrying,' he said. 'It has to me something of the same feel as the boat incident. We may be dealing with something very unpleasant and rather odd. And the last thing we want just now is bad publicity for the society.'

'Oh of course. The new membership drive. Yes, Lavinia would be furious if we scupper that after all the work she's put in. Can I help to clear up then?'

'No thanks. No one else knows where the books and papers belong. I'll have to do it myself. But, if you don't mind, we'll forget the drink. I'll get to bed early and start first thing in the morning. I wish I knew who it was and how

10

he got in.'

'It's a bit worrying.'

'A bit, yes. Thanks for the lift, Ninian, and congratulations on Venice. You did a first-rate job.'

'Thanks. Good night then.' Much relieved at having his offer of help refused Ninian went away.

CHAPTER THREE

He was a scholar, and a ripe and good one.

SHAKESPEARE

Professor Michael Pomfret was sitting among the book stacks on the second floor of the London Library and he had four full days before him of almost uninterrupted enjoyment. It was early autumn and a fine day. Soon he would go and buy a bun and eat it in the leafy garden of St James's Square among the lovers and the secretaries, the shoppers and the art enthusiasts, the holy contingent from St James's Church, Piccadilly, and the occasional politician from Chatham House.

Professor Pomfret was sixtyish, short, thin, frail and ascetic-looking, impeccably dressed and groomed, and displaying all the accoutrements required for the everyday comfort of the very very rich. His family were Old Money from Philadelphia. He always stopped at the Dorset Square Hotel which, because of its position hard by the land which was turned into the first cricket pitch by Thomas Lord in the early nineteenth century, was full of prints and murals to do with cricket and even decked out the younger members of its male staff in cricketing pullovers. This appealed to the professor who had regularly eaten his strawberries and cream and flirted with young ladies in their summer dresses while watching matches at the later Lord's Cricket Ground during visits to London in his youth.

He had hired the hotel's vintage Bentley and its chauffeur to take him to the Library. On this visit his wife had decided to accompany him, rather to his dismay. Emmie had insisted, and when Emmie insisted in just that tone of voice, you got out from under. This morning she had come with him as far as the Library and then directed the driver to take her on to Harrods although her husband pointed out to her that the Bentley was needed for another visitor to the hotel.

'Never mind, dear,' she had said in her flat, harsh Boston voice. 'I'll just get him to wait a little while and then he can take me straight over to the Silver Vaults. I'm meeting Rachel there and we'll be back at the hotel in time for lunch so that will fit in just fine. It's all such a different tempo, isn't it, from back home? Jane

12

Carter told me I'd find it much more leisurely and I didn't believe her. "Jane," I said, "London is a capital city and it must be just as busy and efficient as New York or Washington. I can't believe the tempo is any different." But I was wrong and Jane was right. It's much slower and more old-world. So restful. I could stay here forever. You did get the reservations for Paris, France, didn't you dear?'

'Yes, dear.'

He knew that Emmie would ignore his protest and keep the car and chauffeur just as long as it suited her but he tried to put that worry out of his mind before embarking on the trawling of the bookstacks for the haul that would occupy him so pleasurably for the next few days. But first he must check through the typescript of his talk for RPS in the evening.

The promise to give the talk at the Royal Institution had been given in a rash moment at the Danieli during the May conference. Professor Pomfret was an extremely distinguished Coleridge specialist and a talk by him to RPS would be a very special event.

So here he was wasting the first morning of his time in the Library revising a talk he didn't want to give and for which he wouldn't even be paid. (Such considerations are not lost even on Old Money from Philadelphia.)

The only saving grace about the evening would be the venue. There would be a pleasant feel about lecturing in the very building, perhaps the very room, where Faraday, Darwin and Humphry Davy had lectured before him. Even Coleridge himself had attempted a series of lectures and Byron had gone there to listen to him. These were pleasures that Professor Pomfret particularly enjoyed on his visits to Europe.

Unfortunately, this time such pleasure would be destroyed by the knowledge that Emmie would be sitting there in thin-lipped boredom as he held forth. Then, having already, if he knew his Emmie, made exhaustive enquiries into the composition of the audience, she would push past everyone else in her eagerness to mingle with the members on the way to the reception, intent on forcing herself on the attention of anyone who was famous or distinguished. He sighed and went to get a cup of coffee in Jermyn Street and then to St James's Square with a carrier bag from Fortnum's, leaving his typescript lying on the desk. What could be safer than the London Library?

He came back an hour later to find the typescript had been soaked in red ink so thoroughly that it was indecipherable.

Professor Pomfret's knees buckled under him and he sat down. He felt a little sick. It was so improbable an event. Here in the London Library. The thought that someone inimical and irrational had been lurking somewhere in the building disturbed him horribly. Who had been told that he would be here today? The committee of RPS, the driver, Emmie, and no one else. But no member of RPS could have done such a thing. It must be some madman with a grudge against the Library.

He went to summon help. The librarian was deeply apologetic. He insisted on telephoning the university himself and Pomfret instructed his secretary to fax the original of the typescript to him at his hotel. He then made his way back to Dorset Square. He was too upset to carry on working at the Library.

He told the girl at the desk that he was expecting a fax from the United States and went upstairs. He took off his jacket and shoes, lay down on the bed and loosened his tie. He began to feel calmer.

The door of the bathroom opened and to his dismay Emmie came out swathed in bath towels and turban, lotions and scents, with little screams of surprise at seeing him back already.

'Oh there you are,' she said, 'I quite forgot to collect the key when we came back. Rachel and I had so much to talk about. So the chambermaid let us in. We had a fine time at the Silver Vaults. You'll love the pieces I bought. Look at this, isn't it darling?'

He closed his eyes.

CHAPTER FOUR

Here Wisdom might resort.

COLERIDGE

The early spring meeting of the Coleridge and Other Romantic Poets Society was being held at the Royal Institution. Martin Proctor hurried across Piccadilly as the lights changed, and struck up into Albermarle Street. He loved London and particularly enjoyed this walk.

He passed by number fifty, still the publishing house of John Murray with the room on the first floor where Byron called on his publisher, made the acquaintance of Sir Walter Scott, foregathered with Samuel Rogers and Thomas Moore and regularly borrowed Murray's copy of the *Morning Chronicle* to read its account of the day's proceedings in Parliament. There, a few days after news of Byron's death was brought to England, his memoirs were solemnly and misguidedly burned in the fireplace of that famous room.

Martin walked on, past the little cafés with the couple of token tables on the pavement outside, and then the first of the small art galleries. He passed by the Royal Arcade, resisting the temptation to call in at the bookshop on the corner, and pressed on past the gallery with the one vibrant shocking-pink and green abstract in the window, across the street from which the most proper and restrained of all London hotels was serving delicious nursery teas in a large room full of chintz-covered armchairs, resembling nothing so much as the drawing-room of a rich, elderly, old-fashioned aunt.

Nearing the Royal Institution Martin looked away from the ugly modern building that blocked the view on the far side of Grafton Street and turned in through the glass and mahogany doors of the great, phoney façade on the right. They had painted the columns brown and pink and they looked like Neapolitan ice cream. Inside all was dignity and grace, with black and white squares of the polished floor and the marble chimney piece, its hearth filled with flowers. (Martin never noticed that the flowers were artificial and the effect was fine and welcoming.) On the wall hung the portrait of Michael Faraday gazing commandingly towards the door of the lecture room. The lecture this time was to be unusually obscure and the gathering was therefore rather smaller than usual. Some had come simply to meet their friends and would endure the lecture in order to enjoy the bunfight. You could come for the lecture and leave before the bunfight. But it would hardly be decorous to arrive in time for the latter if you had succeeded in missing the whole of the former.

17

Martin Proctor had warned the lecturer, Harold Kristeller, that the London evenings were designed for the pleasure of the lay members and that his lecture must therefore be comprehensible to a collection of people who, though educated and knowledgeable, were not instructed in esoteric modern methods of interpretation and analysis.

Kristeller had ignored this advice and, when Martin later heard the lecture, he made up his mind never to have this tactless oaf again.

Having taken Kristeller into the lecture room and left him in the charge of Ninian Wallace, Martin returned to the entrance hall to look out for Matthew Frost who, as an entrepreneur, had created a multi-million pound business empire, was a public figure and must be welcomed by the chairman. Frost was patron of the society in fact as well as name. He allowed RPS to use a room in the Frost Building and his secretary, Lavinia Wallace, dealt with RPS affairs with the help of a young assistant. Frost came to most of the meetings and was affable to the members but everyone was aware that he expected to be treated with a certain deference.

However, he was a spirited champion of the society. Whenever he was interviewed he tried to bring the Romantic poets into the discussion and as he was an extremely powerful personality the luckless interviewer often found himself obliged to feign an interest in

Keats or Shelley. This came to be regarded as the relatively harmless foible of a self-made man avid for cultural respectability. Few understood that Frost had become genuinely fascinated with the Romantic era and was widely read. He had also become a collector of some note but this was known only to other collectors.

Martin had already greeted Professor Kenworthy and congratulated him on the publication of his latest book. Kenworthy was one of the most popular members, pursued by the women and liked by the men. His talks were by far the most entertaining but his books were incomprehensible to most laymen and also, it was rumoured, to many of his fellow academics. Those who understood them least praised them most enthusiastically.

Martin was about to return to the lecture room when a large man with a shock of untidy white hair, deep-set, brilliant dark eyes and an unmistakable great beak of a nose came in through the swing doors wearing a long shapeless overcoat and scuffed shoes, carrying a plastic bag full of books in each hand. He stood looking round urgently. Martin recognized him at once and was stunned at the unexpectedness of seeing Léon Bracousse here at a meeting of RPS. Bracousse was one of those seminal figures who had guided the world of letters away from the known routes of literary biography and literary criticism and

19

launched it on a new course. Modern art had divorced art from the common man. Bracousse and his like were engaged in divorcing literary critics from literature.

He was not one of the 'boa-Deconstructors' but a man of equal stature, backed by his followers to be gestating something as original as, and far more sensible than, Deconstruction. No one interested in the study of literature could have failed to recognize him.

What was Léon Bracousse doing here? Martin went forward with outstretched hand.

'Sir,' he said, 'what an honour for the society. I'm very happy to see you here. I'm the chairman, Martin Proctor.'

'Good evening,' said Bracousse in pleasantly accented but fluent English. 'I am sorry to be a little late but London traffic is very bad. May I leave my coat and books somewhere and perhaps my audience will be patient for a few minutes while I wash?'

Martin gulped and stopped himself just in time as he began to say, 'Your audience, sir?'

With scarcely a pause—the military commander faced with a surprise attack—he quietly said instead, 'Plenty of time, sir. Let me take your things.' He led Bracousse to the cloakrooms and to his great relief the great man vanished into the gents'.

No member of RPS had ever seen the dignified Martin Proctor sprint as he now sprinted across the hall and into the lecture

20

room. He clapped a desperate hand on Ninian Wallace's shoulder and pressed the scarf, coat and bags of books into his arms at the same time guiding him out of the room into the entrance hall, much to the indignation of Harold Kristeller who was deserted in mid-conversation.

'Ninian,' Martin said in tones of great urgency, 'it's the hoaxer again. I don't know how it can be possible but he's sent us Léon Bracousse who's under the impression that we've invited him to give this evening's lecture.'

Ninian stuttered, wild eyed, and Martin silenced him. 'Only one thing to do. Take him out to dinner, the Arts Club, just around the corner. Mention my name. Tell him there's a delay. Important guests haven't arrived. Some such tale. On the way you'll have to explain what's really happened. Throw us on his mercy. Tell him the whole story: Venice, my flat, Pomfret's paper covered with red ink. Eat humble pie. Invite him to be chief speaker at the Norman Abbey Conference.'

Ninian looked panic stricken. 'I'm no good at this sort of thing,' he protested.

'Nonsense. You've got to do it. I can't, I've mugged up on Kristeller's subject. The academics may lean on him during questions. No one could handle that who hasn't done his homework on it. Otherwise, of course, I'd take Bracousse with pleasure. It's an honour, Ninian.'

21

'I'm not academic enough for Bracousse.'

'Neither am I. I'd send Kenworthy with you but he's already in there. It would cause a stir. Tell him you regard it as an honour. And find out all you can. Was the letter of invitation on our paper? Has he still got it? That sort of thing. He'll be out of the loo in a minute. Put his coat straight back on him and get him out of here. Go on. RPS depends on you.'

He gave Ninian an authoritative push then walked firmly away into the lecture room and shut the door.

Ninian looked about him wildly and saw a charming figure stealing in through the swing doors, a look of rueful guilt on her delicate features. It was Rosie Finch, probably the youngest and certainly the most nubile of the present membership of RPS. She was swathed in a long black coat which she threw off and flung over her arm as she headed for the lecture room revealing an open-necked, full-sleeved, white silk shirt worn with black velvet trousers. On her finger was a cornelian ring. Rosie did her best to look thoroughly romantic at RPS functions. Her fair curls were tied back with a ribbon and she rather resembled early portraits of Shelley.

Ninian pounced on her and took her hand. 'Rosie!' he said. 'You've got to help. You're coming with me to the Arts Club. We're giving an elderly gentleman dinner. I'll explain later.'

Rosie looked at him apprehensively. 'Me?'

she asked with an uncertain smile. 'You want me to come with you to the Arts Club?'

'Yes please, Rosie.'

'Well, yes, of course I will if you really want me. But why me?'

'Here he comes. Into action, Rosie. You've no idea how much depends on you.'

He advanced on the approaching philosopher and, made courageous by his desperation, gently but firmly inserted him into his overcoat.

'How do you do, sir,' he said. 'I'm Ninian Wallace, the deputy chairman. The chairman has asked me to invite you out for a drink before the lecture begins.'

'But I understood the lecture is to begin at six-thirty and I am late already.'

'Well sir,' said Ninian with a nervous gulp, 'two of our chief guests haven't arrived yet. So we're starting a little late.'

The great man looked puzzled but he said, 'If my audience can wait I would like nothing better than to come with you for a drink.'

'And this,' said Ninian with great pride, 'is Rosie Finch, one of our younger members. She is coming with us. Rosie, this is the famous scholar, Monsieur Léon Bracousse.'

Rosie held out a small white hand and Bracousse raised it to his lips.

'Enchanted,' he said and the hard brilliance of the dark eyes softened as he noticed that the hand was trembling. 'Come then let us go.' He

23

put his arms round both their shoulders and swept them out into the street.

'This way,' said Ninian.

'To tell you the truth,' said Bracousse, 'your invitation mystified me. It will be a pleasure to lecture at your Royal Institution, but do they understand the vocabulary?'

'The point is, sir,' said Ninian, as they turned into Dover Street. 'We didn't invite you to address the society.'

Bracousse stopped dead and turned to him. 'Is this a joke? Your chairman wrote inviting me to speak.'

'It wasn't Martin Proctor who invited you, it was a hoaxer who has been playing tricks on the society. He tried to make it as embarrassing as he could for us by inviting the most distinguished speaker he could think of and asking you to one of our lighter-hearted evenings. We do have academic occasions like the yearly conference and if we thought you might one day agree to come to that we'd be enormously honoured.'

'What an extraordinary thing,' said Bracousse, and they walked on. 'Well, in that case I shall talk to them informally and tease them a little.'

'It's extraordinarily kind of you to take it like this, sir, but it's more embarrassing than that,' and Ninian did in fact look as if he would like to sink through the floor. 'There's an awful complication.'

24

Bracousse stopped dead again and looked at him with raised eyebrows.

'Of course,' he said. The most embarrassing thing he could think of. 'You already have another speaker for tonight. That's it.'

'Yes sir. That's precisely it.'

Bracousse began to laugh. 'Come along then,' he said, 'lead me to the bar.'

Rosie began to giggle nervously and Ninian smiled. By now Bracousse was positively roaring with laughter.

'My poor young man,' he said. 'And your poor chairman! How polite you both were and how well you concealed your horror!'

'If you'll do us the honour, sir, we'd like to take you out to dinner.'

'Splendid!' He seized their arms and swept them along. Ninian guided them into the entrance of the Arts Club.

Two hours later he was hurrying up the staircase of the Royal Institution and across the ante-room with its splendid chandelier lighting up the magnificent portrait of Humphry Davy.

Ninian, bright-eyed, pink-cheeked and under the influence of two sherries, three glasses of claret and two brandies winked at Sir Humphry and hurried on down the corridor lined with scientific tomes and busts and prints of famous scientists. Usually he stopped to examine some of these but tonight he had other things on his mind. He walked into the long library where RPS were eating sandwiches, drinking wine and shrieking at each other at the tops of their voices.

Martin Proctor left Matthew Frost abruptly and came over to Ninian's side.

'Where's Bracousse?'

'He's gone off with Rosie Finch. We gave him dinner and he was quite happy not to speak. He's a very likeable bloke. He saw the funny side of it. Where is Kristeller by the way? I don't see him.'

'I got rid of him in case you brought Bracousse back.'

'A bit high handed aren't you?'

'Have to be, in a situation like this. So Bracousse is painting the town red with Rosie?'

'He's agreed to speak at the Norman Abbey Conference if he can synchronize it with a trip to New York and fly back via London and Nottingham.'

'No! How annoying for our hoaxer! We'd never have thought of asking Bracousse. I'll tell you what, Ninian, we'll have all the publishers vying with each other to publish the proceedings.'

'You don't think Bracousse will frighten some of the members away?'

'Most of them will never have heard of him. We'll simply have to plan the programme very carefully. The big guns in the morning and the *belles-lettres* and so on in the afternoon.'

'What about Kristeller? How did the talk go?'

'He talked the most obscure and pompous drivel. I couldn't understand a word of it myself and Kenworthy obviously agreed with me. Kristeller tried to do a Wittgenstein at the end.'

'What did he say?'

'Something about throwing a ladder away. I heard a great gulp from Kenworthy. Just a little bit irresponsible, Kenworthy, but he'll learn. As for Kristeller, I shan't have him again.'

'He'll be furious. Do you think we can afford to make more enemies just now?'

'We won't have any members left if we put him on the programme twice in six months. Anyway we've enough speakers already for Norman Abbey. Ninian, thank you for coming to the rescue. It was brilliant of you to take Rosie with you.'

'It worked a treat,' said Ninian smiling reminiscently. 'He was eating out of her hand.'

CHAPTER FIVE

I never drank of Aganippe well,
Nor ever did in shade of Tempe sit,
And Muses scorn with vulgar brains to
dwell;
Poor layman I, for sacred rites unfit.

SIDNEY

Sophie Charter rang her former husband, Detective Chief Superintendent John Charter at Penfoldshire Area Headquarters.

'John,' she said, 'I know you're planning to go fishing in Ireland in June. Are you absolutely set on it?'

'No,' he replied cautiously, (he was always suspicious of Sophie when she was cajoling). 'What do you want me to do?'

'Would you consider going to the Coleridge and Other Romantic Poets Society's yearly jamboree instead? It's at Norman Abbey this year and I know you used to be keen on Byron.'

'That's a pretty bizarre suggestion. Why?'

'Because someone has been playing hoaxes on them. It's been going on since last May and one of the hoaxes was dangerous. If they get the police in officially they'll get horrible adverse publicity and they're in the middle of a huge membership drive. They're terrified that the hoaxer will do something to ruin the conference. I thought you might enjoy it.'

'What's your interest in RPS? The head man one of your admirers?'

'As a matter of fact he's trying to pluck up courage to ask me to marry him. I thought you might vet him for me at the same time.'

'You are impossible, Sophie.'

She began to laugh and, much relieved, he said, 'I'll think about it. But if I do go it's only for the hoaxes. I'll have nothing to do with your affairs of the heart.'

'That's marvellous of you, John. I'll tell Martin and he'll ring you and tell you all about it.' She rang off before he could send his love to the children.

Charter considered the suggestion; a series of hoaxes on a famous international literary society, that was intriguing and would be something of a challenge. He could put off Ireland for a few days and enjoy a busman's holiday.

Martin Proctor telephoned Charter that evening and asked him to dinner. 'Can't do it,' said Charter. 'My leave starts the day before your conference. I'll come through London on my way to Nottingham.'

'In that case would you like to meet at the George at Stamford or do you go via the M1?'

'If I'm seriously after your hoaxer and it's a serious problem we ought not to meet *en route* where other travellers in the same direction might see us having a close confabulation. It might make the hoaxer suspicious. This may seem exaggerated but if it is serious we'd better play it by the book.'

'You're right of course. May I give you lunch then on the Friday?'

'I'd rather make it coffee at about ten if you don't mind. I'd like to get out of London early if possible.'

Charter decided to organize some help and telephoned his friend Hartley Godwin at Hangholt Manor.

'Hartley? It's John Charter. I've a suggestion for you. Sophie has bullied me into going to the annual conference of the Coleridge and Other Romantic Poets Society at Norman Abbey.'

'Has she indeed? How the tarnation did she manage to do that?'

'They've got a hoaxer and one of the hoaxes was dangerous. They want me to keep an eye on things. Would you consider coming along? I thought you might find it interesting.'

'Not uninteresting. But just a moment, is it an international affair or just British?'

'International.'

'Then, American academics?'

'Yes.'

'In that case it's out of the question. I'd be strictly *persona non grata*.'

'Now, come, Hartley, that sort of thing got rooted out years ago.'

'No, no, I don't mean they'd be anti-Black as such. It's just me. I'm not politically correct.'

'Well, I don't suppose I am either.'

'You don't get the point, John. I'm a black man. A politically incorrect black man. That's anathema to them.'

'I see. You mean you're not feminist and all that?'

'I'm not in favour of positive discrimination in favour of Blacks. That would really get up their noses.'

'Would they know?'

'I'd make sure they did.'

'Pity.'

'Let me know how you get on. And watch out for the feminists.'

*   *   *

Three weeks later Charter and Martin Proctor were sitting on the balcony of Martin's flat, the strong aroma of coffee fighting the exotic scent of jasmine.

Martin told Charter the story of the sinking of the motor launch in Venice followed by the burglary in London, the destruction of the papers in the London Library and the invitation to Bracousse to speak on an evening when another speaker had been arranged.

'The Venetian episode could well have been an Italian matter,' Charter said. 'I can get in touch with the Italians on that and see what conclusions they came to. The burglary could simply be coincidental. The other incidents were annoying but relatively harmless.'

'We'd thought it was all over,' Martin said,

'when nothing happened between September and February. But he'd been biding his time. As soon as I realized that, I thought of the conference at Norman Abbey. We're inviting the bigwigs from the district and at least one of the local mayors to a reception on the night of the conference dinner. The perfect situation for an embarrassing incident. That's why I felt we needed professional help.'

'Did you ask the distinguished speaker who never got to speak, whether he had answered the letter inviting him?'

'Ninian asked him and he said he did reply.'

'So someone in your office suppressed the letter of acceptance?'

'I'm afraid it looks like it.'

'Where is your office and how many people have access to it?'

'We have an office in the Frost building in Cork Street. Matthew Frost lets us use it rent free. He says it's his equivalent of the Saatchi and Saatchi Art Collection. Ninian and I go in from time to time for meetings. Members can drop in when they're in the West End for Sothebys or Irish House or what have you. And Browns Hotel, where some of our American and Japanese members stay, is just around the corner. The secretary is there full time as she works for Matthew Frost. Lavinia Wallace, Ninian's wife. Frost goes in himself, of course, and so could any of his staff. The place must often be unmanned, especially in the lunch hour, so in theory anyone could call in at the Frost building, walk into our office and pretend to have lost his way if he was found there.'

'And, presumably, he could find out anything he needed to know about your programme and addresses of members, names of boat firms you dealt with on the Italian trip, names and addresses of speakers. So almost anyone could have got hold of the information needed for carrying out the hoaxes.'

'I suppose so.'

'Lavinia Wallace could have done it, though she'd have to be as thick as two short planks to think she could get away with it in the long run.'

'I don't think she's that.'

'Matthew Frost himself might have managed to keep a close enough eye on the post to do it himself. But we're not much further, because anyone other than those two would have given the visiting intellectual the wrong address for his reply. Do you know of anyone with a reason for animosity against the society or you or any other member?'

'I've given that a lot of thought and the answer is no.'

'I can't see then that there's any likelihood of my spotting this character during a five-day academic get-together at Norman Abbey.'

'But you might stand more chance than Ninian or I do of spotting any new hoax. The conference is a gift for the hoaxer. Imagine all those priceless objects in the collection.'

'The Abbey must have their own security to take care of all that.'

'Of course. There's the custodian and the two young women who keep the collections. And all sorts of alarms and panic buttons. But as I don't intend to mention the hoaxer to them I feel bound to provide extra cover myself.'

'Where am I staying?'

'I've booked you into the North of Trent in the Abbey grounds. It's an hotel owned by Matthew Frost who, by the way, will be with us for Saturday morning of the conference. Then he has to go back to London to look after some visiting clients. He'll be back as soon as he can on Monday or Tuesday. He's a northerner and talks a lot about the change in the attitude of English people to one another once they cross over the river. North of the Trent, it seems, there's nothing but kindness and perfect accord, so when he decided to open an hotel at the Abbey he called it the North of Trent. He then gave it to his daughter, who runs it with the intermittent help of the son-in-law, who is bone idle and dishonest too.'

'Dishonest?'

'He was given a suspended sentence for forging a cheque ten years ago.'

'That could be significant?'

'The hoaxer? Oh no, I don't think so. He doesn't know anything about the society.'

'One might check whether he was in London

at relevant times. He too could have got information from the office.'

'Too risky. Lavinia would have recognized him, and Matthew Frost is his father-in-law. I'll see you at the North of Trent.'

'How will you explain my presence among the top brass when I have absolutely no Romantic credentials?'

'You can be my cousin, if you've no objection.'

'Fine. That's all settled then.'

'I'll tell Ninian who you are.'

'That's the man who dealt so tactfully with the disgruntled academic?'

'Under instruction from me. Yes. He's a good deputy but he'd be no good as head man. He's devoted to the Romantic poets though.'

'Aren't all your members devoted to the Romantic poets?'

Martin paused for thought.

'No,' he said. 'Most of the academics think it's hilarious when Ninian or Victoria Tallent want to spend a whole evening discussing Byron's foot. He was lame, you know,' he added, as he noticed Charter's look of surprise.

'Do you find it hilarious?'

'Not particularly but the point is it's completely taboo among fashionable academics. You can't go in for that sort of thing if you want to be taken seriously.'

'So what must you go in for?'

'Philosophy of language. Structuralism,

Deconstruction, Marxism, Feminism, jargon of the most impenetrable kind, the thorniest possible road to nowhere.'

'But you don't envisage that sort of disagreement as having anything to do with the hoaxes?'

'Oh no. We agree to differ. No animosity at all. Well, no strong animosity. Not strong enough to lead to the sort of thing that happened in Venice and here.'

With each succeeding sentence he sounded less convinced of the truth of what he was saying.

CHAPTER SIX

Proving absurd all written hitherto,
And putting us to ignorance again.

BROWNING

At about the time Charter left St John's Wood Minnie Powell set out for Nottingham from Ledgeworth University. She drove a powerful Mercedes into which she had crammed four of the group of students who were accompanying her to the conference. The car was clean and polished but Minnie herself looked scruffy to a degree which was hardly outdone even by her young followers.

Minnie was what is known as a charismatic

personality. She exuded self-confidence without, on the whole, giving the impression of complacency. She was brilliant and articulate but she often resorted to semi-literate diction, her conversation enlivened with scatological remarks, rude epithets and slang. Her colleagues at Ledgeworth had long since become used to this rather unpleasant method of communication. It resembled after all the usage of many of the students they were instructing. But it gravely shocked many outsiders who were still under the impression that Departments of English Literature and Language were places where the young were instructed in the felicitous use of the English language.

Ten years earlier, before Minnie became famous, she had been invited to lecture to RPS as an up-and-coming young academic with startlingly original ideas on the study of literature. In those days she had not yet perfected her rebellious persona. Although a feminist she had not yet decided that the whole field of human knowledge and enterprise must now be reinterpreted and re-evaluated from the point of view of the Women's Movement. RPS found her an interesting speaker but questioned many of her remarks. This led to a lively discussion during which Minnie refused to be crushed. Everybody went home pleased and exhilarated and slightly more open minded than they had been before (which in a few cases was not saying much).

Since then Minnie had become famous for her iconoclastic views and lectured on the need for transforming the study of literature into direct political action. RPS was now anathema to her, for she had abandoned literary criticism as such and was dismissive of those who still believed in it. Her students were exhorted to give up the study of the writers of the past. Instead of waiting until they had received instruction themselves they were to instruct others.

Minnie was far from going in for direct action herself and led a comfortable existence teaching and travelling. Her students had a fairly easy time of it too as they were not expected to read much besides Minnie Powell. The result of these methods of instruction was a stream of partially literate English Literature graduates from Ledgeworth, many of whom soon joined the ranks of the long-term unemployed.

Minnie herself was in the enviable situation of receiving job offers from universities all over the English-speaking world. She was so popular with students of every nationality and geographical situation that the Department of English Literature and Language at Ledgeworth University (which should by now have been known as the Department of Marxist Feminist Revisionist Politics) was bulging at the seams. Universities at this time were in dire need of expansion to retrieve or maintain their financial situation and for the last few years had been vying with each other to poach Minnie from Ledgeworth in the hope of luring a huge influx of students in her train.

In the normal course of events nothing would have induced Minnie to attend a conference run by RPS which stood for everything of which she now disapproved. But when she heard that the great man, Léon Bracousse, was inexplicably leaving his Provençal farmhouse to lecture at Norman Abbey she applied to join the society and arranged to bring a party of her disciples with her to the conference. Bracousse was lecturing on the first day so Minnie planned to leave after the day's proceedings to join her domesticated husband and four well-brought-up children at their country house for the rest of the weekend.

She arrived at the Abbey late in the afternoon, drove to the bed and breakfast farmhouse which had rashly agreed to put up the four students, then returned to the North of Trent, arriving just as a large coach drew up outside.

*   *   *

Dermot Finn arrived at the North of Trent soon after Minnie Powell. Finn was a successful and moderately well-known

39

freelance journalist who had become involved with the Romantic poets when doing a piece on a well-known author who was travelling in the footsteps of Coleridge gathering material for a coffee-table book. After a humiliating experience on Doe Crag (the result of a severe attack of vertigo) he had caught up with this lady at the Palace in Malta and the result was a short sharp love affair which turned out as embarrassing for Finn as an earlier episode at the same venue had been for Byron, both ladies expecting at a later meeting the fulfilment of the protestations made to them during what the gentlemen had later persuaded themselves was no more than a holiday romance.

The later success of the coffee-table book inspired Finn with the conviction that the Romantic poets might prove mildly lucrative and he made a point of covering them whenever he could. He spent two days in Venice during the RPS conference but left before the incident of the bomb in the boat, otherwise there would have been no possibility of keeping that incident out of the English newspapers. He did a tongue-in-cheek piece on RPS for the *Chronicle*'s Sunday supplement consisting of interviews with Greek, French, German, Japanese and Italian members of RPS illustrated with photographs of RPS emerging late at night from the Venice Theatre, of Rosie Finch looking characteristically vulnerable in a gondola with a palace and a prison on each hand and of Lavinia Wallace in chiaroscuro gazing up at the equestrian statue of the *condottiere* in the Campo San Giovanni e Paolo (which appears in Byron's play *Marino Faliero*) the light from a nearby lamp playing on her long, smooth, pale-auburn hair.

Later he went up to Grasmere for a Wordsworth exhibition and walked round the lake in early morning mist with several admirers of 'The Lakers' (as Byron rather rudely called Wordsworth and his friends). Through this visit he became involved in a book collectors weekend at the same hotel during which he met the president of RPS, Lord Hellvellyn, the elderly poet of the Lake District who wrote very dull and derivative blank verse published in handsome editions with water-colour illustrations, and made a very good thing of reading it to Women's Institutes and poetry societies. Hellvellyn had called with his wife and sister-in-law (who was responsible for the water-colours) at the lakeside hotel where the book collectors were gathered and had agreed to allow Finn to buy him a drink while his ladies got on with the real business of the visit (the distribution of pamphlets advertising his readings and books of verse, much to the annoyance of the book collectors who were mercilessly button-holed by these formidable ladies).

Finn suggested doing an article on Hellvellyn, interviewed the two ladies and

41

promised to send a photographer to take pictures of the poet and the famous dog, cat, goat and canary, at the Grange near Ullswater.

Finn arrived at the North of Trent by car and headed for the bar where he found a pleasantly flirtatious old lady who remembered him from Venice, called him to her side and bought him a stiff whisky.

They were joined by Martin Proctor, the Wallaces and an ex-student from Ledgeworth who was now a builder. Then the door opened and in walked Detective Chief Superintendent John Charter of Penfoldshire Constabulary. Finn was startled into silence. What sort of malefactor could Charter be after in the ranks of the lovers of the Romantic poets? Surely none of them could be drug-runners or money-launderers or burglars or conmen? Was there a scoop on the cards? Or was it something to do with the society itself?

'Finn!' said Charter.

CHAPTER SEVEN

Ere Babylon was dust,
The Magus Zoroaster, my dead child,
Met his own image walking in the
garden.

SHELLEY

At midday on that Friday, Mrs Victoria Tallent walked along the platform at St Pancras Station with the help of a silver-handled walking stick, bound for the Norman Abbey conference.

Nearly eighty-two she thought of herself as no more than middle-aged and often referred to less energetic people twenty years younger than herself as 'the poor old dears'. She was still open minded to an extraordinary degree, full of ideas and projects and still capable of putting many of them into practice. Over many years she had done vast amounts of research into the lives of Coleridge, Shelley, Byron, Keats, and even Southey and Leigh Hunt. Her knowledge of locations and relationships and the most distant connections of these poets was encyclopaedic. She was interested not only in the poets but also in their descendants. She had visited dull houses in Ealing where Lady Byron had lived for a time during her long lonely years of self-justification. She had travelled to

Brighton to have tea with a descendant of Shelley and to visit a school where his publisher had once sent his daughters. She had located the tomb of Scrope Davies in the cemetery at Montmartre and invited the society to drink champagne at its base during one of their forays to Paris. She was convinced that such exertions would eventually bring to light an undiscovered letter from Coleridge, a scrap of poetry by Keats, one of the copies of Byron's memoirs. But she felt such studies were worthwhile in themselves and she took great pleasure in them.

Arrived at Nottingham, Victoria took a cab and asked the driver to drive slowly as they turned in past the great Pilgrim's Oak and drove towards the Abbey as the ten-year-old Lord Byron had been driven with his mother and his nursemaid when they travelled down from Aberdeen to take up his inheritance. Victoria always tried to imagine she was that child when she came this way and saw the scene which must have been so exciting for the small Scots boy—the wide stretch of grass, the long low wall of the gardens and then the magnificent soaring ruin of the Abbey church with the glassless Gothic window and beyond it the pale stone of the west front of the house looking out towards the two lakes and the road that went up the hill towards Annesley.

The North of Trent Hotel looked out on one side towards the Abbey and on the other directly down on to the Upper Lake whose waters stretched across to a rim of trees on the opposite bank, and beyond them a rose-red slope of plough, misted over with green. At the lake's edge stood the second of the two forts which had been built in the early eighteenth century by Byron's predecessor, the wicked Lord Byron who had killed all the deer and cut down all the trees on the estate to spite the son who then died before him. It was 'wee Geordie Byron' from Aberdeen who inherited the stripped estate.

The North of Trent had pointed gables, Gothic windows, and a garden full of flowering shrubs and climbers. The taxi driver turned in under the archway and drove into the stableyard depositing Victoria beside the steps leading up to the main entrance to the hotel which was flanked with pots filled with pansies.

A girl came out of the door looking harassed. She wore a shirt and jeans and rubber riding boots. Her straight dark-blonde hair was caught back carelessly in a pony-tail and loose strands floated round her face. The sight of the old lady clearly gave her no pleasure at all though she forced a smile of greeting. Victoria, who was nobody's fool on such matters, was not deceived.

The girl said, 'You must be one of RPS. I'm so sorry. I wasn't expecting them until later. Let me show you your room.'

'Don't you worry, dear,' said Victoria, 'I can

see that you're busy. I'll just sit somewhere quietly until you're free.'

The girl seized her case and led her into a large hall with an open fireplace filled with spring flowers. Chintz-covered armchairs and sofas stood about the room with small round tables, Pembroke tables and woven rugs.

'Would you like tea?' asked the girl.

Victoria lowered herself carefully into a chair.

'Yes, dear,' she said, 'if it isn't too much trouble. I expect you're Matthew Frost's daughter.'

The girl smiled and her grey eyes crinkled under the thick black brows. It was a wide mouth and the face was not particularly pretty but she held her head high on a slender neck.

'Yes,' she said. 'I'm Corinna Tierney. I'm sorry to be in such a rush but Andrew seems to have disappeared, so I was going to have to exercise both the horses myself. They're stabled you see so it's got to be done no matter what. But luckily for me one of your people arrived even earlier and I was so horrified to see him because I'd sent the staff off until four that he offered to exercise with me. So he did, and he's rubbing them down for me now. The staff should soon be back and I'll send Jean in with tea for you and John Charter. Will you be all right till he comes in?'

'Of course I will. You're very like your father.'

46

'Am I? I'm flattered. He's supposed to be rather dishy. Do you know him well?'

'He's been to my house. I showed him my research on the Lamb family. Who is John Charter?'

'He says he's a cousin of the chairman.'

'He can't be. Martin Proctor hasn't got a cousin.'

'Well never mind. I'll just see if Jean's there.'

As the doors to the kitchens swung to behind her the front door opened and a tall man with thick dark hair, a longish face and bright blue eyes with slightly drooping lids came in. He used a boot jack to remove his riding boots, put them neatly by the door and walked into the room stretching and yawning, rubbing his eyes and pinching his nose like a very tired man. He paused on catching sight of the old lady swathed in Indian cotton and silk jersey hung with silver chains and bangles, her shining hair carefully waved. Little curls escaped and floated round her forehead.

'Oh good afternoon,' he said. 'I didn't know the party had arrived.'

'You're supposed to be Martin's cousin,' she said. 'He hasn't got a cousin.'

'Not a real cousin,' replied Charter with great aplomb. 'I'm a courtesy cousin. I assure you I'm not going to steal the silver.'

Victoria smiled. 'That's all right then,' she said. 'Are you going to join the society?'

'I rather doubt it.'

47

'I'm Victoria Tallent,' she told him, and they shook hands. 'Corinna tells me you went riding with her. Where are the gee-gees?'

He came and sat down beside her. 'I'll take you to see them later if you like,' he said. 'They're in the stables which means a lot of work for our hostess who seems a little overworked as it is. They are stabled to keep them fit enough to go in for events. The husband likes competing on them.'

'She's a lovely girl,' said Victoria who thought everyone young was lovely. 'Do you know her father? He's a very clever businessman though he makes some mistakes. But he doesn't know much about the Romantics. Don't tell him I said so. He wants to be invited to speak to the society.'

'I don't know much about the Romantics myself,' said Charter. 'I've been reading them up a bit over the last few weeks. I became very Byronic at school but it didn't last.'

'Shelley's the one,' said Victoria. 'Read Shelley.'

'I don't like Shelley,' said Charter firmly. 'The only bits of Shelley I like are the bits that don't sound like Shelley.'

Victoria looked at him disapprovingly but over scones and cherry cake they became very friendly indeed. Then Charter removed his feet from the low stool on which they were comfortably resting, pushed the tea trolley out into the kitchen and brought the housekeeper

48

back to show Victoria to her room. He then went up to his own and after indulging in a prolonged soaking in a hot bath he dressed and went downstairs. Some time earlier he had heard the arrival of the bus from London but now no one was about.

He went out of the front door, through the stableyard, under the archway, and walked along near the quiet lake, his eyes on the west front of the Abbey now touched with a pale apricot bloom by the last glow of the sun. Lights shone from the upstairs windows. It was very peaceful. He turned away and sauntered along the road that went past the cataract that shot out from the lake down to the brook that fed the Lower Lake, and on up the hill. Two figures were walking down towards him at a fast pace, striding along hand in hand, their longish hair blowing in the light wind that had sprung up with the evening. They looked like a couple of young lovers, their faces turned towards each other so that they seemed to be leaning into the wind and leaning at the same time towards each other. There was an extraordinary impression of tension about this attitude.

As they passed by they turned and said good evening in unison and Charter was surprised to discover that they were old—a tall, powerful-looking man with white hair and lined and haggard face and a younger but still elderly woman wearing a light woollen coat that flew out behind her. She was very thin and her eyes were deep set. The man wore a cloak and carried a walking stick. They strode away round the edge of the lake and headed for the North of Trent.

CHAPTER EIGHT

By my troth, captain, these are very bitter words.

SHAKESPEARE

Charter followed the couple back to the hotel and found many of the guests drinking in a bar overlooking the lake. Victoria was holding court with a large whisky in front of her and five men gathered round her, one of whom was the journalist, Dermot Finn, a short, thickset man of about forty with sparse, curly greying hair and an expressive ugly face.

'Come and sit next to me, dear,' Victoria called as she saw Charter and he came and sat opposite her next to Finn.

'Finn,' he said, 'how good to see you—on holiday no doubt and incognito.'

Finn noted the minatory tone and answered with a smile, 'That's right, Charter. Exactly so. You too?'

Charter gave him a sideways glance. 'What are you after, Finn?'

50

'What are you?'

'Nothing, Finn.'

'Well I'm here to interview that old maniac, Hellvellyn.'

'So that's who it was! I saw him out walking with a lady friend.'

'Not a lady friend. He's looked after too well for that. He daren't make a move without his wife or her sister to keep him on the straight and narrow.'

'He's a bit old, isn't he, for straying off it?'

'No one's ever too old, take it from me.'

'I thought Hellvellyn shunned any sort of publicity.'

'Those are the keenest to be interviewed.'

'Well, take note. There's no story.'

A short, thin, crew-cut American leaned over to Victoria and asked, 'Put up any good blue plaques lately, Victoria?'

'No,' said Victoria and the American, Harold Kristeller, laughed. Victoria looked at him crossly and Kristeller smiled rather acidly.

Ninian Wallace took up the cudgels for Victoria.

'It took her years of hard slog to make them put up the plaques and we ought to be grateful to her,' he said.

'Oh, but I admire her energy,' protested Kristeller. 'One has to face it that there are loads of people who are entranced with every minute detail about the lives of their heroes, even to the point of seeking out uninteresting houses that are difficult of access and very far away, just to visit a place where some distant connection of the poet once had tea. They revere the patio where Mary Shelley hung out Shelley's socks to dry and the privy in some country garden where Byron's aunt—'

'That will do,' said Martin Proctor. 'I seem to remember you joining very happily in just that sort of activity when you first joined the society, Harold.'

'What's more,' said Finn, 'Victoria's motives are pure and yours are venal.'

Kristeller gaped at him.

'You academics know that unless you jump on the latest bandwagon you'll lose your jobs.'

Kristeller went dark red and walked out of the room.

Martin turned on Finn angrily. 'That was totally uncalled for,' he said.

'Aren't we all venal?' said Finn comfortably.

'Kristeller's a bit edgy,' Ninian said. 'He expected to be asked to give a paper.'

'I'm glad his expectations were disappointed,' said Finn. 'I've heard him on television and that's to say I know everything he's likely to say or write for the foreseeable future.'

'Finn!' said Martin. 'Don't cause trouble.'

'If I do,' said Finn with a smile, 'you'll forgive me when you see the nice things I write about you in the paper.'

A youngish man came into the room playing

a drum roll on the hotel gong with a consciously charming smile. He was handsome and sun-tanned and his hair was expertly cut and blow dried. Charter's heart sank as he realized that this must be Corinna's Andrew. This character had left Corinna to exercise two horses (one of which was kept for his pleasure) on a busy day. Andrew Tierney looked a thoroughly shady character, and rich men's daughters married to shady characters have a hard time of it. He liked Corinna and the thought that she was probably still working over a hot stove and would presently have to change in a hurry, annoyed him.

Martin had organized a table for himself and Charter, Professor and Mrs Pomfret, the two walkers by the lake (who turned out to be Lord Hellvellyn and his sister-in-law, Miss Cunningham) and Lady Hellvellyn, who was a shorter plumper version of her sister. Charter found himself placed next to Lady Hellvellyn with an empty place on his left.

Lady Hellvellyn leaned over to fix Charter with an autocratic eye.

'You've read my husband's poetry?'

'I've read his letters to *The Times*, Lady Hellvellyn, but I'm regrettably ignorant of modern poetry.'

'He doesn't write modern poetry. He is the Romantics reincarnated.'

'I'm not tremendously knowledgeable about the Romantics either.'

'Then what are you doing here?'

She turned her shoulder to him and engaged Martin Proctor in conversation.

Charter decided to pump Professor Pomfret on the perplexities of the academic world at the present time.

'Professor,' he said, 'I've been told it's war in the universities between those who study the poets as well as the works and those who think that is outdated. I see your lecture tomorrow is to do with the relationships between the poets. Are you challenging the people who think that background is irrelevant?'

The professor turned to him, the light of battle in his eye. 'Ah,' he said, 'you've heard that they tried to destroy my papers at the London Library. You're quite right. They do attack me and tomorrow I shall be defending myself. We disagree on almost every aspect of criticism today. I'm a mimeticist (I believe literature should reflect reality). They attack mimeticism. I believe in the study of literary works. They want to throw all that out because they say it's outdated and irrelevant. I believe in qualitative difference; some books are better than others. They challenge even that.'

'A tabloid newspaper as good as *The Winter's Tale*?'

'Yes. They even talk about the death of the author.'

Charter burst out laughing. 'But not, I assume, the demise of the literary critic. What

54

on earth do the authors make of it?'

'Most of them pay no attention. That's the crass stupidity of it. They're relegating criticism to an ivory tower. And then we have the masses of untutored fanatics who preach political correctness to their elders and betters. Before I left the States I received an impertinent letter from a young woman newly employed by the publishers I've been dealing with for thirty years, instructing me to go through the manuscript of my new book and change every "he" to a "he or she" and every "his" to a "his or hers". Next they'll be attacking and persecuting great authors whose works they disagree with. They've already persecuted some academics out of their jobs. But I have a project I hope to be engaged on very soon. A project that will prove the worth of traditional studies.'

Professor Pomfret's colour had risen and his hands were trembling. Then he turned politely to Miss Cunningham and Charter turned back to Lady Hellvellyn whom he found with her eyes fixed on Emmie Pomfret in what looked remarkably like jealous rage. Emmie had discovered that Hellvellyn was a baron and was flirtatiously trying to prevail on him to explain to her the correct forms of address. Miss Cunningham too was gazing anxiously at Emmie and her brother-in-law. Lord Hellvellyn, it seemed, was guarded by his two elderly ladies from all possible contact with female marauders. Charter wondered why they took the trouble for Hellvellyn seemed unmoved by Emmie's advances. He concentrated on his plate and more or less ignored her.

Miss Cunningham now favoured the whole company with a description of her walk with Hellvellyn. Apparently what Charter had witnessed was not an evening stroll out from the hotel and back, but the end of a four-hour walk from the village where all three had spent the previous night, Lady Hellvellyn accepting a lift from friends since she was not strong enough to walk so far.

Altogether it seemed a consciously appropriate set-up for a reincarnation of the Romantic poets.

Corinna slipped into the place next to Charter and picked up a glass of mineral water.

'My dear,' he said, 'have some wine. I thought you'd never come.' And he poured her some Mosel. Her hair was limp, her face flushed, the thick brows knit and the expression tense and strained.

'Don't worry,' he said, 'the food's delicious. You're doing well.'

She looked up at him and smiled. 'It's kind of you to say so,' she said, 'but I know it's good. I'm a professional and I'd never serve anything that wasn't. But I get no time to do my face. I look terrible. I don't know where Andrew's been but all the things he should have looked after I've had to do.'

'You look fine.'

'Don't lie.'

'I'll rephrase that. I like the way you look.'

'This frock is awful.'

'I like awful frocks.'

She laughed and began to eat. They all began to congratulate her on the food and the flowers and the rooms and Corinna talked and smiled and Charter, watching her, wondered why he was beginning to fall for a harassed young woman with a husky voice and no particular beauty.

Later, Andrew presided in the bar and Charter led Corinna out into the garden where several people were sitting in the warm dusk looking out across the lake water.

'How well do you know the top brass of RPS?' he asked, trying to keep his mind on the problem in hand.

She shook her head. 'I only know Martin and Ninian and Lavinia. My father once took me up to Windermere to meet the Hellvellyns.'

'Your father is interested in Wordsworth and the rest of them is he?'

'He's gone completely overboard about it. He tried to bring us up as if we were landed gentry and we're not. We're quite ordinary. He decided that to impress people he must become an authority on something. He had some false starts but it's been Byron for some time now. He's been working at Melbourne Hall mugging up something so he can give a talk to RPS himself. To prove he's not a Philistine. As if anyone could care less. He doesn't have to pretend; everyone respects him for the qualities he already has. Do you know, I think we'd better go in. I can't be sure Andrew won't go off and leave the bar unmanned.' She led him back towards the bar and as they reached the door Andrew came blundering out, red-faced, eyes too bright, clasping a plump and pretty young woman by the hand and dragging her along with him.

He wavered when he saw Corinna but she took no notice of him. She glanced at the girl who was very young and said kindly as they went by, 'It's getting cold out there, Daisy. Make him get you a pullover.'

The girl went scarlet and Andrew muttered something that sounded like 'bitch'.

Charter swung round on him but Corinna took his arm firmly and Andrew went on unscathed, Daisy now hanging back and dragging her steps.

Charter drew Corinna into the empty hall.

'Tell me,' he said, 'how does your Andrew get away with being such a sod? Isn't all this yours?'

'That's why he behaves like such a sod. He can't forgive me for it.'

'Will you stay with him?'

'I don't know.'

'The instinct for self-preservation seems to

be missing.'

'I don't like giving things up once I've taken them on.'

'He won't change.'

'I want to make a success of the hotel and I couldn't manage alone.'

'Yes you could, and your father would help you.'

'How do you know? You've never met him.'

'It's inconceivable that he wouldn't. He must want to get you away from that character.'

'We don't talk about it.'

'It's time you did. Why on earth did you marry him?'

'I was very young. He was very handsome and I thought he was charming.'

'I suppose he still is handsome though the charm is not in evidence tonight.'

'No he isn't.'

'Isn't what?'

'He's beginning to get that slightly seedy look some men get when they begin to lose their looks. It's going to make him unhappy. Beautiful men are terribly vain.'

'Aren't beautiful women?'

'No. They get their vanity knocked out of them because men are so nasty to them. Look at Lavinia Wallace. Ninian is so rude to her. She's so lovely. You'd think he'd be proud but he's not. People are much kinder to you if you look like me. They think that beauty is

59

enough.'

'And isn't it?'

'It must be very gratifying but it can't be enough.'

'No I suppose not. And men don't have the same experience? I mean women are nice to beautiful men.'

'Yes. Look at me. I was a complete fool over Andrew. Daddy knew it but I wouldn't listen. Look, we'd better go in.'

So they did.

CHAPTER NINE

You who in different sects have shammed,
And come to see each other damned;
(So some folks told you, but they knew
No more of Jove's designs than you).

SWIFT

In his room Charter reviewed the situation. Could he picture one of these people as the hoaxer?

Andrew Tierney had disappeared for the afternoon when he was supposed to be helping Corinna. Was that significant? He doubted it. Corinna had treated it as normal.

Professor Pomfret had shown that he was feeling embattled but if he was irritated at RPS for inviting Bracousse, he proved himself innocent of being the hoaxer. The hoaxer knew that RPS had not invited Bracousse. And the top brass at RPS seemed to share Pomfret's distaste for what was going on in the world of letters. In any case the hoaxer's campaign wasn't the sort of thing Pomfret would be capable of setting up unless he had roped in an accomplice.

Then there was the silent and morose Lord Hellvellyn, guarded and pampered by his solicitous companions. If his poetry could be described as the reincarnation of the Romantics it was probably dismissed as pastiche by the critics. So he might well be in the same case as the professor, angry and defensive. But his wife had admitted that he wrote derivative verse and that didn't seem to her to detract from its value. Hellvellyn might take the same view.

Then there was Martin. Of all the people he had met so far Martin was the one with the necessary qualifications for carrying out the hoaxes. He had been in the army. He was efficient and self-confident and had the necessary information and access. But he hadn't the slightest reason for damaging RPS as far as one could see.

Ninian Wallace? Might have a motive— jealousy of Martin Proctor. But he didn't seem dynamic or inventive enough. Nor did Lavinia.

Next morning he was up at seven but was not

61

the first in the dining-room. A large, white-haired man in a polo-necked pullover, shabby flannel trousers and ankle-high mountain boots was laughing over a copy of the *Daily Mail* with a fair-haired girl in a full-sleeved white shirt and black trousers. Charter went to a table by the window where he was joined by Martin Proctor.

'As your cousin,' he said, 'I shall breakfast with you. Have you made any progress?'

'We'd better not overdo the cousinly relationship,' Charter told him. 'Mrs Tallent tells me you haven't got a cousin. Not much progress I'm afraid. It's obvious that there are stresses and strains in the academic world. Perhaps some academic has developed an irrational animosity to RPS. But I don't believe the answer lies there. The organizing of the hoaxes took energy and foresight. The motive must be a very pressing one. I don't think academic rivalry would spark off such a long drawn-out affair.'

'Oh I don't know. Some of the academics are regular prima donnas.'

'But the majority of them are very pleasant rational friendly blokes. And all these ones here seem to have booming careers.'

'Not quite. Look at Pomfret. He doesn't want to retire for years but his department has climbed on to the Marxist/Feminist bandwagon, where he doesn't want to follow. Then Kristeller. He's got to publish but he's

62

got nothing to say. He could do a popular book but that wouldn't count towards his career, though he might make a bob or two. So he's trying to learn the jargon and go in for a bit of mystification. Dreadful mistake. Kenworthy's doing all right but he's got a first-class mind.'

'What about Hellvellyn?'

'A joke. His poetry's a joke. He gets invited to read it to obscure literary societies and it sells quite well to the sort of people who read light verse.'

'You're a snob, Martin. If he has that sort of audience for it you can't say his poetry's a joke.'

'The sister-in-law's water-colours are remarkably good. Most people buy the books for the illustrations.'

'Does that upset him or doesn't he know?'

'The only thing that would upset him is if they failed to sell.'

'Why is he here?'

'He's our president.'

'What about your deputy chairman as hoaxer? Is his nose out of joint at being a mere deputy?'

'Ninian? Never. He may resent me but he's tremendously loyal to the society and so is his wife.'

'Who works in the Frost building and actually in the office Frost gives to the society.'

'She would never have written that letter.'

'Even if her husband had asked her to?'

'They aren't exactly devoted to each other.'

'I see. Well, what about you?'

Martin looked astonished briefly then nodded. 'Yes. Of course. It could all be a tremendously subtle double-bluff. Do you see me as the hoaxer?'

'As an ex-military man, however short your service may have been, the organization of the hoaxes, and particularly the attack on the boat in Venice, would come easily to you. Were you SAS by the way?'

'No, I was not. But I could perfectly well have put that charge in that boat. I suppose I should be glad you're doing such a thorough job. If I had done it myself I'd be kicking myself now for bringing you in.' He seemed rather amused by the idea.

'I suppose,' he went on, 'we can rule out Mrs Tallent.'

Charter smiled. 'If we found a suitable motive for that old lady I'd certainly look for a *modus operandi*,' he said.

'Are you coming to hear Bracousse?'

'I'll come to some of the lectures to get the feel of the thing but I'll start by going over the Abbey defences.'

'They should all be there today. It's the first time they've let anyone in like this. They won't let us upstairs except for the reception tonight which will be thoroughly policed. They've got a priceless collection up there. Apart from that we'll be in the Orangery. Are you going to do a recce round the park too?'

'I've done that already. I went riding with Corinna yesterday. We went as far as Annesley where Byron's girl-friend lived and she told me about the hill with the diadem of trees where they used to meet and how the poem about it was read later on all over Europe and the husband went with an axe and cut all the trees down in a rage.'

'To tell you the truth I can't concentrate even on the hoaxer at the moment. This conference is unlike any conference we've ever had before. We've made a terrible mistake in having Bracousse.'

'He seems rather pleasant.'

'It's just that because we've got him we've got far too many of the firebrands. Minnie Powell would never have come if we hadn't had Bracousse. And when you get Minnie you get all the rest of them.'

'Who?'

'Oh I don't know—the Feminists, the Marxists, the Feminist Structuralists, the Marxist Psychoanalysts, every brand known to man of Post Modernist, the Black Feminists—but of course,' he added conscientiously, 'I don't object to them. Or to the others as long as they behave themselves. But they won't like our programme which has nothing to do with sexual politics or female sexuality or cultural politics or sexual textual politics or the Marxist Feminist Literature

Collective.'

'It's just as well then. If they don't like your programme they won't come again.'

'But they'll upset Professor Pomfret and tell him he's a Recalcitrant Humanist. And my talk at the banquet won't appeal to them at all. It's all about Erasmus and Humanism and good will among scholars of all nations.'

CHAPTER TEN

*The times were bad, the Saints had
ceased to reign!
A few yet lived to languish and to mourn
For good old manners never to return.*

CRABBE

Charter went out of the hotel and found Rosie Finch sitting disconsolately on the steps.

'Aren't you going over?' he asked. 'You'll miss Bracousse's lecture.'

She looked up at him with tears in her eyes. 'I don't want to go to it,' she said. 'Léon doesn't care a bit about Shelley or Byron or any of them. He thinks everything people like me and Victoria think important is just novelettish. It upsets me. I can't help it.'

'My dear girl,' said Charter. 'Don't pay the slightest attention to his views on literature. These geniuses have lots of fun with their

66

theories but that's got nothing to do with the rest of us. We're perfectly entitled to admire *Little Women* or *Ouida* if we want to. Bracousse's theories only matter to other geniuses.'

'Then you don't think I must go to his lecture?'

'Come and show me round the Abbey. I've got to see the custodian first but then I'll be free. Meet me by the front entrance in twenty minutes. I know very little about Byron: you can instruct me.'

'Well if you're sure.' She was radiant with pleasure.

'Twenty minutes then.'

Charter went round to the side door of the Abbey and rang a bell. After a long time an elderly man let him in.

'I'm sorry,' he said, 'we're busy fixing a surprise for the conference. Only unfortunately it seems to be the main topic of conversation among them already. We're using hose pipes to fill up Byron's plunge bath with water. What can I do for you?'

Charter explained that he had been sent by Martin for instruction about the security system, produced his warrant card as evidence of good faith and underlined the need for secrecy about his calling. Then the custodian showed him round and talked to him about the Abbey's defences.

He said, 'If you don't want to set off the

67

alarms you can't breathe round here once the system has been connected.' And he proceeded to demonstrate the accuracy of this remark so thoroughly that Charter went back to meet Rosie convinced that the hoaxer wouldn't stand a chance of embarrassing RPS by depredations on the collection unless he proved to be one of a sophisticated gang of criminals provided with the best equipment on the market.

Rosie was waiting for him and they spent half an hour walking round the Abbey. As they came to the cloisters she said, 'Come on! Let's see if it's true that they're trying to fill the Slype with water.' She took his hand and led him along past the chapel next to which a heavy door stood open. She leaned forward to look down into the dark sunken passageway which had long since been blocked off and roofed over. Several hose pipes were steadily pouring water onto the stone floor which was already some feet deep in clear cold water.

Then they went to the Buttery and she made a detour to show him the tree on which Byron and Augusta, his half-sister, had carved their names before she went back to her ne'er-do-well husband and he up to Seaham to his strange, stiff, priggish bride and where in the kitchens of Seaham Hall the wedding cake had gone mouldy because the reluctant bridegroom had tarried too long.

As they went into the Buttery where coffee

was being served, Professor Pomfret came out and paused to say, 'If you want to hear a first-rate speaker don't miss Kenworthy. Unfortunately I'm about to call a cab to take me to Southwell. I've arranged to collect some sterling from the bank so I mustn't be late. I believe the banks shut at twelve on a Saturday.'

'Let me drive you there,' said Charter and failed to notice a look of great reproach and disappointment from Rosie.

'Well it does take time to get a taxi,' said Pomfret. 'Thank you.'

They drove into the small town of Southwell past the Minister and the Saracen's Head and the professor directed him to the car-park behind the Inn. As he drove along the narrow path they had to stop and reverse to allow a grey Jaguar to come out. The driver waved his thanks and Charter swung round to look at him. He was almost sure that it was Matthew Frost, whose features were well known from his frequent appearances on newsreels and business programmes on television.

Professor Pomfret went off to the bank and seemed to be away for a very long time. Charter ordered sandwiches in the bar and met Andrew Tierney coming out, his arm round the waist of Daisy Masters. Twenty minutes later the professor returned clutching under his arm an oblong package wrapped in brown paper as well as the briefcase he had been carrying all morning.

'Can you call me a taxi?' he asked. 'I'm sorry. I intended to give you lunch, but I find I have to make a quick visit to Melbourne Hall. Now, don't offer to drive me there. Get yourself something to eat and get back to the conference.'

Within five minutes Charter was seeing the professor into his taxi.

The professor leaned out of the window and said, 'Don't mention Melbourne Hall. Mrs Pomfret might be disappointed. She rather likes making private visits to places like Melbourne Hall. One wouldn't want to break in on the family, particularly as the whole party is invited there for tea today.'

'You can rely on me not to mention it,' said Charter, surprised to see that the professor appeared to feel no embarrassment at this revelation of marital discord. He was probably so used to making arrangements of this sort to avoid arguments with Emmie that his sensibilities were blunted.

Charter drove back to Norman Abbey and spent some time prowling round the crypt, cloisters and gardens. There was no sign yet of the hoaxer but today was the most likely day for him to make some sort of move.

As he headed back to the Orangery for the lecture, Professor Kenworthy overtook him carrying a pile of books and papers. He was a young man in his early thirties with a square jaw, high cheekbones and a large round head

70

thickly covered with dishevelled mousy-coloured hair. He had a friendly manner and his rather small blue eyes crinkled into laughter at any excuse.

'Are you one of us academics?' he asked.

'No,' said Charter, 'I'm here on sufferance but looking forward to being instructed.'

'Well this'll be a good one. Come on, I daren't be late, I'm chairing this session.'

Charter stepped forward to open the door of the Orangery for a young woman. To his astonishment, Kenworthy now pushed rudely past the woman and swept Charter into the room ahead of her.

Kenworthy gave him an amused sideways glance. 'Don't say a word,' he said. 'I'll explain later. Got to rush,' and he hurried across the room to his place next to Professor Pomfret. Kenworthy sat down and turned the microphone towards himself.

'Well,' he said, 'here he is. The man you've been waiting to hear. Professor Michael Pomfret, one of the foremost authorities on Coleridge but perhaps even better known for the extraordinarily illuminating comparative studies which have dealt so sensitively with the relationship with the other Romantics.

'What you may not know is that for the past ten years Professor Pomfret has been engaged with several people in the UK on the setting up and financing of free Universities behind the Iron Curtain to help the academics and

71

intellectuals who've had no access to Western thought for more than a generation. This has built up immense good will and could be considered his most important work.'

Pomfret made disclaiming gestures but a look of great pleasure came over his face as the audience applauded enthusiastically.

Charter was surprised at the authority Pomfret took on as soon as he began to speak. His delivery was excellent and he spoke with humour and humanity. When he ended he was rewarded with applause which was polite but not as enthusiastic as the reaction to his work in Europe.

Minnie Powell was immediately on her feet. Her question might have been in a foreign language as far as Charter was concerned. He recognized the word mimeticism which the professor had explained to him and it was clear that she was accusing Pomfret of naiveté. She was greeted with loud applause from her claque.

Pomfret's hands were trembling. Kenworthy glanced at him and took up the challenge himself. Then they were at it, hammer and tongs, Kenworthy raising a laugh from one section of the audience, Minnie eliciting noisy applause from another. In the end Kenworthy made a gesture symbolic of a bang on the table with a gavel and said, 'I think we must continue this at our leisure, Minnie, and give this audience the chance to put their questions to the professor on his paper.'

Martin Proctor asked a question about the literary value of Coleridge's play *Remorse*. The professor answered briefly. Kenworthy then kept a firm hold on the proceedings and firmly squashed two of Minnie's students who tried to put provocative questions.

As they trooped out of the Orangery and along the cloisters to the crypt and the front entrance, Charter saw Kenworthy stepping back courteously to allow Rosie Finch to go ahead of him. Charter shook his head at him and Kenworthy laughed and walked along beside him. 'No harm at all in opening a door for Rosie,' he said, 'but you were risking life and limb. That woman is one of the most implacable feminists in the business—Miss Eleanor Hershey of Crashaw University. Don't ever open a door for her.'

'Thanks for the warning. But surely Crashaw's Ivy league?'

'The worst of the lot.'

'I enjoyed the lecture.'

'Oh yes,' said Kenworthy. 'Old Pomfret discovers nuances that are totally illuminating.'

'Above the head of Minnie Powell?'

'No. That's what's so mischievous. Minnie appreciates every nuance but won't admit it. She's an interested party. She's for the underdog and she claims that the study of the literary canon is unfair to him because it's elitist and Eurocentric and phallocentric (so unfair to women) and it's used by the Establishment to keep the underdog in his place. What with Minnie and the Bracousse lot, who are into theory rather than practice, it's a poor look out for Pomfret and his sort.'

'I still don't understand why Pomfret was so upset.'

'He's used to people like Minnie at home but he's never had to put up with this sort of thing in this country before. We always treat him with the respect he's earned during a long career. But his own university are among the worst. They probably want him out of his Chair.'

'And who would they put in his place?'

'God knows. Certainly someone politically correct, chosen by the thought police.'

'American thought police! And I thought Minnie Powell would be risking her career by attacking such a distinguished man.'

'Not long ago you'd have been right. Now it's the reverse. Pomfret was sticking his neck out by delivering a traditional piece of criticism with Minnie in the audience. Moreover, he offered some remarks which Minnie and her people would regard as rank anti-Feminism. That's rash to the point of idiocy, though in his defence I have to say that I don't think for a minute that he'd have done it in the States—at least not at his own university. At a normal RPS conference, (which this is definitely not), he could say anything under the sun and we'd defend to the death his right to say it. But we don't usually get Minnie and her gang at an RPS conference.

'Mind you,' he added, 'poor Minnie has her cross to bear too. She's what known to the self-righteous as a Tenured Radical and they think you can't get much lower than that.'

As they came out into the fresh air, Martin was standing by the door of a large bus, a foot tapping angrily.

'I'll dump my books,' said Kenworthy. 'See you on the bus.'

Charter walked over to Martin. 'Anything wrong?' he asked.

'You are coming to tea at Melbourne Hall aren't you? I booked a bus big enough to take the whole conference. You'd think they'd be interested. There are the paintings and books and the Norman church and the mill pond and the gardens. But Minnie is leaving and the whole of her contingent has refused to come. Look at them.'

Charter looked at them sprawled on the grass with their cans of Coca-Cola and their Walkmans.

'I don't see any harm in it,' he said. 'They probably prefer sunbathing to culture?'

'I wouldn't mind if it was just idleness but it's a rebellion. They say Melbourne Hall and its gardens is a symbol of the eighteenth-century subjection of women so they are making a political point at the expense of the owners of the house who have catered for all of us.'

'Was it wise to book for everyone?'

'Well of course it was. We go to see these places in a party. Occasionally a few people decide not to come with us but we've never had a rebellion like this before.'

'RPS are usually more docile are they?'

'You need some co-operation when you're organizing a conference like this. Lots of people would give their eye-teeth to drink a cup of tea and eat a bun with Lord and Lady Ralph Kerr.'

'I wouldn't be surprised if that's what your rebels object to. Martin, has it occurred to you that the people involved in your rebellion are the very ones who aren't particularly fond of RPS and this little contretemps gives them plenty of scope for a hoax while you're away? So, no, I'm not coming out to tea. I'll go over to the hotel and make sure no one can tamper with the food.'

Martin looked aghast.

'Well,' said Charter, 'you don't want headlines in the papers about food poisoning and everyone having the gripes and throwing up at an RPS conference. And it would pretty well cut short the rest of the proceedings. An obvious hoax I'd say. By the way I think I saw Matthew Frost in Southwell this morning.'

'Are you sure? I thought he'd be here. He's got to get back to London later today.'

'Does he drive a grey Jaguar?'

'Yes he does.'

'It was him all right. Perhaps he was checking up on his son-in-law who was there with a lady.'

'If I were Frost I'd have punched him on the nose and brought him back with me.'

Charter looked at him in surprise. This was a new aspect of Martin's character.

'That would have done more harm than good,' he said. 'Go on and enjoy yourself.'

Martin climbed wearily into the coach.

CHAPTER ELEVEN

Offend her and she knows not to forgive.
POPE

Charter watched the party get on to the coach, Kenworthy dashing up at the last moment. Then he walked across to the North of Trent to find it deserted. In the kitchens everything was ready for a fast-moving operation to prepare the food and transport it over to the Abbey. Bowls of washed lettuces stood in ranks, large white dishes were laid out with portions of marinading steak covered with muslin nets, dishes filled with strawberries stood beside a mass of serried avocadoes. He should have realized that preparations for such an

77

operation would start early in the day. It was possible that he was already too late.

His job now was to make sure that no one came in to tamper with the food before Corinna's team came back to deal with it. No one came in until Corinna herself walked in in her white coat, followed by her helpers.

Later, having changed into dinner jacket, he walked past the room next to his own and paused as he heard voices raised inside. The door burst open and Emmie Pomfret stood on the threshold looking back into the room with a look of utter venom on her face.

'You spoil everything,' she shouted, too angry to recognize that Charter was behind her and that everyone within two storeys could hear her voice. 'I don't know why I came to Europe with you. I'll have much more fun going on widows' cruises when you're dead and I wish you were, I really do. The first time you've ever brought me to a conference and you won't even escort me to the dinner.' Emmie slammed the door, gave it a look of blind fury, and flounced down the stairs.

Charter said good evening to her as she hurried past him and she paused, composed her face and gave him an attempt at an ingratiating smile.

'I'm so looking forward to the banquet,' she said. 'Are you going over to the reception now? I'm afraid my husband isn't feeling well tonight and he won't be joining us.'

'I promised to walk over with Victoria Tallent,' he told her. 'She isn't very steady on her feet.'

'I'll see you later then,' and she went out of the door, her mouth hardening to a thin, red line.

Victoria came down a few minutes later and they set out on the slow walk across to the Abbey. Lights shone from all the windows and poured out of the door to the crypt. They followed the other guests who were making their way to the South Staircase leading up to the Great Hall. Ahead of them a girl in black and white culottes and a neat black silk jacket was striding along swiftly, carrying camera equipment in both hands. She had short, silky blonde hair. She was tall and slim and purposeful. She was Sophie. He couldn't leave Victoria and Sophie was too far in front for him to call to her in less than an indecorous bellow. Martin must have asked her to take the official photographs. To his surprise he failed to feel the leap of the heart that was his usual reaction to an unexpected meeting with his former wife and this worried him. He must be more involved with Corinna than he had realized and that mustn't be allowed to develop into anything important. More than anything in the world he wanted Sophie and the children back. But all the same he knew that he was waiting impatiently for the moment when Corinna would slip quietly into the place

79

beside him, push her hair out of her eyes and let him pour her wine.

In the Great Hall, Lord and Lady Hellvellyn, Martin Proctor, Ninian and Lavinia Wallace, stood in line by the door to welcome the guests. Victoria paused to talk to Lady Hellvellyn and Charter walked on and looked for Sophie. She was already taking shots of people coming into the room. She gave him a friendly smile but waved him away so he went on into the cloister galleries, found the custodian and asked permission to prowl around the collection. Then he went downstairs again to patrol the crypt and the cloisters where several young waiters and waitresses were now setting out trays on long tables covered with white tablecloths placed against the wall near the chapel and the Slype. A large portable cassette player stood at the end of the table nearest the chapel. Corinna came hurrying in to collect her staff.

'Hello,' she said. 'We've got to drop everything and get on upstairs. The mayor wants to see the whole staff.'

They trooped up the stairs and Charter followed them just ahead of the party of local dignitaries, Press and photographers.

After the mayor's speech and Martin's reply, Corinna gathered her staff and ran downstairs on the heels of the departing mayor. Charter followed more sedately with Victoria.

Everyone invited to the dinner processed

along through the crypt and cloisters. Flares on the walls sent moving shadows across the stone floors, up the walls and the glassed-in cloister windows. The Mary Garden and the stone fountain in the middle of the cloister-garth were in darkness, quite shut off.

Ahead of them people were lingering, clustered round the door to the Slype. There was some clapping. Burning flares were taped to the rail that ran round the walkway half-way up the walls. The lights shone on the surface of the clear, cold water through which you could see the magnified outlines of the stones which made up the floor.

In the Orangery, Corinna had candles and vases of white daisies on every table. Lord and Lady Hellvellyn, Martin, the Wallaces, Bracousse and Rosie Finch were installed at the top table (the first time the lovely Rosie had ever graced a top table at any function). Emmie Pomfret was there apologizing to Martin for the absence of her husband, who had evidently stuck to his guns in spite of Emmie's wrath. It seemed the ostensible reason for his absence was an attack of gastritis.

Having led Victoria to her place Charter found his own which was near enough to the top table for him to have an uninterrupted view of Sophie being firmly led by Martin to a place at his right hand. Sophie was remonstrating with him but Martin silenced her by pointing to the single pale pink rose that lay across her place-setting. Sophie's expression changed as Martin spoke. 'It's yours,' Charter heard him say. 'It's a new rose and it's called the Sophie Saltram. They've sent six bushes of it to the Mill House for your garden.'

Sophie went scarlet and hid her confusion by lifting the rose and plunging her nose deep into the furled petals. She picked up the scroll that lay beside it and looked at it briefly. 'I don't know what to say,' she said gruffly, then all the top table gathered round to admire the rose, casting sidelong glances at Sophie, who they now suspected might become first lady of the society. Martin smiled happily as Sophie thanked him stiffly, quite unaware that with the gift of the Sophie Saltram rose he had probably destroyed his chances with Sophie forever. Charter happened to know that the gesture must have cost Martin several hundred pounds. So much the worse for him. If Sophie knew this it could only make matters worse. She hated being put under an obligation.

Charter found this episode puzzling.

Either Martin felt very sure of Sophie indeed, in which case Sophie's reaction once they were out of public view would show him how wrong he was, or it might mean that he hadn't got to first base with her and was resorting to desperate measures in order to do so. There was such a lack of common sense in making so public a gesture without first making sure of Sophie's reaction that he began to wonder whether Martin was as level-headed as he seemed.

Sophie now firmly went to pick up her camera. Attention was further diverted from the pink rose by a cry from Emmie.

'Look what those men are doing!' she shrieked, pointing towards the much enlarged copy of Giorgione's *Tempesta* which hung on the wall near the cloister door. 'That picture must be worth millions!'

Two young men in jeans and leather jackets were standing on chairs in order to remove the painting from the wall. Nobody was paying the slightest attention to these proceedings and if Emmie had not cried out they might have taken it out of the room without a dissentient voice. They had no such intention. Having set the painting carefully down they turned it face to the wall.

Martin strode across the room.

'Just what do you think you're doing?' he asked in an outraged voice.

They gestured towards Miss Hershey, the young woman from Crashaw University who was advancing on him with a conciliating smile.

Martin turned to her.

'Don't worry, Martin,' she said. 'We're not making any affirmations yet about the offensiveness of the painting. If they want to hang it here on exhibition that's fine. But you must understand that the display of a female nude in an academic situation does really constitute sexual harassment. So we want it taken down for the duration of the conference. You don't want to give offence to the women here do you?'

Ninian Wallace was by this time at Martin's shoulder.

'You have no business to touch that painting,' said Martin. 'And there is no one here who could possibly be so crass as to take offence at it.'

'I've discussed it with my colleagues,' said Miss Hershey. 'We do take great offence at it.'

'But, Miss Hershey,' said Ninian, 'the woman is feeding her baby.'

'Stark naked and with that man in armour looking on. We consulted together and made our decision. It will be quite safe with its back to the wall. After all, Martin, it isn't the original.'

Martin drew himself up with a thunderous brow. 'Its value,' he told her, 'is beside the point. I doubt whether either of us is competent to make a judgement on that. Your action is embarrassing for the society. We have given guarantees; nothing is to be touched. I shall seriously consider putting this before the international council. We're lucky the painting isn't wired up to the alarm system. Put it back. Now. And be careful. Any damage might cost Miss Hershey dear.'

The two young men looked at each other

and Miss Hershey, turned back to the wall, climbed on to the chairs and put the painting back in its place amidst loud applause, catcalls and whistles from different sections among the audience. Martin cast an outraged glance round the room. Such behaviour was quite foreign to the proceedings of the Coleridge and Other Romantic Poets Society.

Miss Hershey was now red in the face and bridling.

'You are giving great offence to the Women's Movement,' she said.

'Bugger the Women's Movement!' From a table nearby came the voice of Dermot Finn.

'I apologize for that remark,' said Martin hurriedly. 'But that's what you get when you behave so—like this. My late wife was a feminist and I can tell you she would have been horrified at such petty-minded nonsense. This is a work of art, Miss Hershey, and not a piece of propaganda.'

Then he turned away and called in an irritated voice for everyone to be seated. The waiters and waitresses came in from the cloisters.

CHAPTER TWELVE

... Well said, old mole! canst work i' the earth so fast?

SHAKESPEARE

At the top table, Rosie Finch was drooping over her tournedos. Kenworthy and Bracousse were talking to each other over her head and Charter had no doubt at all that what they were talking was shop. Kenworthy was excited and every so often he burst out laughing. Bracousse was deeply interested, his eyes fixed on the younger man, a half smile on his lips. They looked like lovers. Rosie clearly understood not a word they were saying and they were oblivious of her.

Before the speeches Charter went out into the cloisters and walked around to check that all was in order. The waiters were removing the table they had used for serving the food. He went upstairs to check with the security men. As he returned to his place he saw that Dermot Finn was scribbling quietly in a notebook on his knees, his eyes busy watching the top table and following Charter's return.

He sat down wondering what Finn would write about RPS and whether they knew what they were risking in inviting this friendly, clever man who was completely without scruple once he sat down at his computer and began tapping out his stories and comments and judgements about other people.

The coffee cups were whisked away and the waiters brought in brandy and liqueurs. One of them carried in the tape recorder Charter had seen in the cloisters and placed it in front of Martin. Then he went out and shut the door.

After Martin had delivered his chairman's graceful speech of welcome and thanks he switched on the cassette player to play the customary messages from absent members of the society. This year, he told them, there were messages from Prague, Hiroshima, Boston, Bologna and Moscow.

A deep voice began to speak and Martin sat up, frowning. This was no university professor from Prague. It was an uneducated voice and it spoke loudly in a monotone that was somehow alarming quite apart from the words it uttered.

The voice said, 'Listen very carefully, all you nobs. It's the Poets Society I'm talking to and you'd better listen if you want to live ...' Martin leaned forward and switched the machine off, his face suffused. 'I'm sorry,' he said, 'this must be a practical joke. Someone has switched the tapes.'

There was a silence then Emmie said on a high note, 'No, Martin, you must put it on again. We want to know what he's going to say. It's frightening.'

Martin switched on the tape again and it

went on, 'You've drunk your coffee and guzzled your food. Now the waiters have gone and we've wired both doors up. If anyone opens the door there'll be a very big bang. And some of you won't live to tell the tale. You won't get any help from the security guys. And why? Because we've done the same to them. So you'll stop where you are until eight a.m. if you know what's good for you. After that the wires will be OK. Right? Don't go near the doors. Got it? Have a nice evening.'

Charter met Martin's eye.

'Is it true?'

'What do you think?'

'Wouldn't think so for a moment if it weren't for the boat in Venice.'

Charter turned to where Corinna sat nearby.

'But the waiters will be coming back for the coffee cups won't they, Corinna?'

'No, they won't,' she said. 'It's going to be so late. I've let them go off. We'll clear up first thing in the morning.'

Charter went to Martin's side.

'May I talk to them?'

'Of course.'

He turned to face the room and clapped his hands to quieten the hubbub.

'Ladies and gentlemen,' he said, 'I'm an expert on this sort of thing so I must ask you to trust me and do as I say. I would like to be able to assure you that this is only a hoax but it might just not be. It's possible that someone is engaged in some plan to burgle the collection here and this could be their way of keeping us all out of the way. It's very tedious and unpleasant for everybody but it isn't dangerous as long as everybody does the sensible thing. We must keep away from the doors.'

He walked over and stood in front of the door to the cloisters. After a moment Ninian Wallace got up and went over to the second door.

'Now,' said Charter, 'I know the idea of stopping here all night seems absolutely grotesque but it's better than risking someone getting hurt. We'll find ways of making everyone as comfortable as possible so I suggest you finish your brandies while we have a council of war and see what we can work out. There's just a chance that I might manage to get you out through the windows so don't despair.'

'Oh God!' called Rosie Finch in a trembling voice. 'It's just like that awful Buñuel film *The Angel of Death* when the *dolce vita* people get stranded at a party for days and days. It was horrible.'

'Ah yes,' said Dermot Finn in his soft, yet carrying voice. 'I wonder whether there's a cupboard in this room where we can place some large utensils for the relief of the company as they did in the film.'

Martin gave him a look of fury. 'Don't make

it worse than it is,' he said sharply. 'We'll be out by morning whatever happens.'

'Martin,' said Charter across the room. 'I want to investigate the locks on the windows. Will you take my place over here while I have a look round?'

'Of course.' As Charter went over to the window Martin walked towards the door. He was delayed by Emmie Pomfret who caught his arm as he moved away. 'Martin!' she said. 'What about Michael? My husband. What if he decides to come and join us after all? He might come to look for me and set the bomb off.'

Charter turned back and his eyes met Martin's in dismay.

Meanwhile a figure had risen from a table near the side of the room and was making its way slowly towards the door to the cloisters. It was Victoria Tallent. On occasions like this, when several people were gathered together, a moment often came when she removed her hearing-aid to give herself a rest. Consequently she had heard neither the tape nor the subsequent discussion.

Charter suddenly realized that she was going to open the door and that it was unguarded. With a warning shout he flung himself across the room and wrapped his arms around Victoria's knees in a rugby tackle, at the same time endeavouring to guide her bulk so that it fell across his body which would break her fall.

He was too late. The door swung open as

Victoria collapsed on top of Charter. Someone screamed. But there was no explosion.

Martin had thrust Emmie aside and rushed after Charter and he now went gingerly through the door and examined it and the door jamb. He came back into the room smiling widely and said cheerfully, 'It looks as if it was a hoax and we'll all sleep in our beds, but don't touch the doors till we get the security men down to have a look.'

Someone laughed on a high, nervous note. Corinna, Finn and Ninian carefully lifted Victoria on to her feet. She rummaged in her handbag as they held her up, found her hearing-aid and pushed it in. 'That's better,' she said. 'What happened? Did I fall?'

'The doors were booby trapped,' Finn explained gently. 'John Charter tried to stop you.'

'Booby trapped? Who would do such a silly thing? Well thank you, dear, for saving me from a wetting.'

Finn shrugged and smiled and by common consent they told her no more.

'I expect it was that Powell woman,' she added as they put her tenderly back in her seat. 'She's a real hussy that one.'

Sophie came up and said, 'Come on, I'll take you to the loo. It's quite safe now.' And she led Victoria out of the room.

Charter got to his feet breathing rather fast. 'Martin I'm going to check with the security men that everything's all right up there. Will you see that no one goes near the doors till we come down?' he said, and went in search of the men whom he found drinking coffee in the Great Hall.

'Tell me,' he said, 'have you by any chance had a message about a threat to wire up the Orangery with explosives?'

They said in unison 'No', and looked their surprise.

'It's a hoax,' he told them. 'And the likeliest motive for that must be burglary, though I have to tell you that I don't think it's that myself. But if I were you I'd get on to your local police at once. And I want one of you to come and check the other side of the second door out of the Orangery. There's no wire or explosive to be seen on the cloister door but we can't assume anything about the other one until we've checked.'

Once they had done this Charter went straight to impound the tape recorder and the tape. The machine was still there, but when he pressed the eject button he found the compartment empty. Someone had removed the tape. He could have kicked himself. Here was firm evidence and he had lost it. He took Martin on one side.

'Look,' he said, 'I'm sorry. It's the very thing you got me in to prevent but I'm afraid there's nothing for it now, we've got to call in the police.'

Martin looked at him calmly. 'Yes,' he said. 'He's won.'

'Yes, I'm afraid he has. I know you don't want the publicity. But we've got to stop this joker. He's getting more and more irresponsible. We might have a real disaster. The other possibility is that this is tied up with a plan to burgle the Abbey.'

'So do we all wait here for the police?'

'I'm afraid we do. But they'll be here within minutes and we'll be allowed to leave very soon after that.'

Within five minutes a team of police officers arrived. Charter decided not to introduce himself to his colleagues at this stage. All they had to do was to make sure that the collections were safe and this they did with admirable dispatch, searching the buildings and the gardens, checking with the custodian and the hired security men, taking names and addresses, impounding the tape recorder, finding out when the conference would be breaking up and who would then be leaving the country and asking everyone to be available for questioning in the morning if necessary. Then they were all given the go ahead to go back to their hotels.

As Charter waited he thought about what to him was the greatest puzzle about tonight's events. Why go to all the trouble of setting up so elaborate a hoax rather than put something mildly toxic into the food? And the answers he gave himself gave him no comfort.

It was two hours before the Abbey settled down again. The doors were locked and the alarm system switched on again. The police went back to their headquarters leaving a PC on guard.

After doing his bit ferrying startled elderly ladies back to the North of Trent, soothing everyone in sight, putting an arm round a drooping Corinna with a reassuring hug and helping Sophie to carry her camera equipment back to the hotel, Charter went back for a last look at the Abbey. Finn, who had been walking by the lake, came to join him and they stood looking up at the dark windows and the arch of the great priory church window black against the sky. A light breeze had come up and the bright moon was half hidden by ragged wisps of cloud-wrack.

Finn shivered. 'Can't you feel them gathering about?' he said and Charter turned to give him a hard stare.

'Who do you think is gathering about?' he asked.

'The powers of darkness,' said Finn and smiled at him. 'It's the Celtic faculty of seeing things that others can't see,' he explained. 'Brought on no doubt by over-indulgence in Courvoisier late at night.'

They walked slowly over to the North of Trent and Finn seized the opportunity of putting many questions to Charter about his mission here at Norman Abbey. And Charter gave him no answers.

CHAPTER THIRTEEN

... now the bat
Wheels silent by, and not a swallow
twitters,
Yet still the solitary humble-bee
Sings in the bean-flower!

COLERIDGE

Charter went to sleep at once but slept fitfully. At 2.30 he got up and looked out of the window. Now the night sky was cloudless. A breath of scented air came up to him from the garden and a cool breeze lifted the hair on his forehead. He was about to turn away and get himself a drink from the room bar when he swung back and peered into the darkness. Beyond the broad undulating band of bright reflected moonlight that spanned the Upper Lake was a different sort of light—a glow that came from behind the fort at the lake's edge. It kept dying down then flaring up again. It was a bonfire and someone was regularly feeding it with fuel or possibly burning something on it bit by bit. His mind turned to the red ink poured over Professor Pomfret's paper at the London Library. Burning some of the papers to be given at the conference would be a coup for someone with a grudge against RPS.

He couldn't rouse Martin or Ninian as he had no idea where their rooms were. He must do this on his own. He pulled on a T-shirt, shorts and sneakers and went out of the window. Using the thick stems of the wisteria as an extra hand hold he went down the drainpipe by his window, across the shadowy garden, over the wall, down the sloping shore and, kicking his shoes off, into the lake. He went into a fast crawl that took him across the lake into the bright path of the moonlight and on in to the dark waters under the trees on the opposite bank.

Seizing an overhanging branch he pulled himself up out of the water and scrambled up the bank. A shadow fell across the ground in front of him, a twig cracked behind him and a blow struck him on the back of the head. He fell to the ground.

A voice was saying querulously 'Bloody fool' and repeating it monotonously and irritatingly again and again as he reached down and dredged himself up out of a deep lethargy. It was his own voice whispering exhortations to himself. Bloody fool to let the hoaxer knock him out. He'd warned Martin that the fellow was dangerous. Just as well he wasn't on official business or he'd look a sorry fool.

He lifted an aching head. In front of him was something large and dark that blocked his

96

view. There were soft rustlings and scutterings all about him and somewhere far away a fox barked. He shook his head and a sharp pain jabbed at him behind the eyeballs.

His arms were stretched out in front of him and he flexed his muscles and found to his astonishment and fury that his wrists were tied together. He tried to pull them towards him and came up against the trunk of a tree. His arms had been placed around the tree-trunk and the wrists roped tightly together.

There was no sign of his assailant who had presumably scarpered. It wasn't long before Charter began to suspect that the man had tied him up with a quick release knot. It took him five minutes to get enough purchase to undo it.

He got slowly to his feet and leaned his head against the tree-trunk, clasping his arms around it for support. Soon the sickness and dizziness cleared and he began to walk cautiously about and came to the edge of the lake. His eyes became focused on the band of moonlight through which he had swum and he remembered the bonfire and turned to look for it. The glow had been extinguished. Stumbling, he started to walk towards the fort behind which the flames had shown and in the faint light from the moon he searched the ground as thoroughly as he could, his head throbbing and aching every time he bent down.

He found the site of the fire but the glow had been smothered and the ashes kicked away, or possibly thrown into the water. The ground must be searched again in daylight. He walked carefully back to the lake and stumbled along the bank until he saw some flotsam floating on the surface, went in to the water up to his thighs, gathered up the floating pieces of charred log and waded out again, clutching his finds to his chest. Then he carefully placed the heap on the ground, took off his T-shirt and managed with some difficulty to tie it all up safely. He then began to trudge painfully home around the edge of the lake.

He hurried across, shivering, to have a word with the PC on guard at the Abbey's entrance, who had seen no sign of movement either near the North of Trent or in the Abbey grounds. Charter went back to the hotel and up the drainpipe to his room, untied his parcel and examined the bits of flotsam. To one of the pieces a trace of charred paper still adhered. He took out the plastic laundry bag supplied by the hotel and put the flotsam into it, closed the bag with a twist of plastic, lay down on the bed and reviewed the situation. He ruled out burglary from the collection. No one would steal something valuable only to set it on fire. This was RPS business and the man on the opposite bank of the lake was almost certainly the hoaxer. But in the morning he must go at once to talk to his colleagues at police headquarters.

CHAPTER FOURTEEN

As cold as any stone.

SHAKESPEARE

Charter woke in a rather cheerful frame of mind. The bomb scare and the bonfire presented an interesting challenge and he was rather sorry to have to let the local police share it. He joined Sophie at breakfast just as she was finishing her coffee and when Corinna came in to take orders for breakfast she got up to leave.

'I'll leave the field to your girl-friend,' she said and Charter looked at her sharply. It was said with a smile but there was a trace of animosity in Sophie's tone. She wasn't pleased at his interest in Corinna and that was being dog in the manger indeed. Nevertheless he smiled.

He half stood up as Corinna came towards his table but as she saw him she looked him straight in the eye unsmiling and went out again. One of the girls came out of the kitchens to take his order. For some reason Corinna was angry with him and he couldn't think why.

He headed for the kitchens as soon as he had dispatched the bacon and eggs. Corinna was there conferring with her staff. He waited leaning against the wall with his hands in his pockets. She finally turned round, gave him a blank stare, and went out of the room into the private wing.

A thought struck him and he went through into the hall where the Sunday papers were laid out on a table. Sure enough, Finn had done it. There on the front page of the *Chronicle* was his own face. The caption was *Chatty Charter Hunts a Hoaxer* and the sub heading, *Sardonic Super Rubs Shoulders with Eggheads*. (Charter was ironically known to the Press as Chatty Charter because of his extreme taciturnity when being interviewed.)

Here was the reason for Corinna's behaviour. He thought about it. She had welcomed him as a helpful guest, ridden with him, talked to him about her problems, allowed him to give her advice. Now she had learned that he was a policeman incognito. She felt deceived and betrayed and he couldn't blame her although to have told her the truth would have been a betrayal of Martin's confidence. He had lied to her and everyone else. Looking back, had he not received some unfriendly glances in the dining-room? And yet, last night, they had happily put themselves in his hands when he offered expertise over the bomb scare. He had been a policeman long enough to accept the irrationality of such reactions.

All the same he cursed himself for not having foreseen that Finn would ignore his warning. On the whole a journalist would try to keep on the right side of any high-ranking police officer he happened to know. But in this case the story had been too good to miss.

Finn had exercised his wit at the expense of RPS citing the Venice story but not the case of the London Library or the invitation to Bracousse. No doubt the members were still gossiping about the Venice incident and Finn was past master at possessing himself of the latest gossip. The other two incidents were known only to Martin, Ninian and Rosie. Even without those incidents the story was a good one. Finn described the literary dilettanti, the dons, the overseas intellectuals, the feminists and the noble poet from the Lake District huddled together at Norman Abbey waiting for the next attack by the hoaxer. He told the story of the bomb scare and made it sound hilarious, bringing in Buñuel. He described the hoaxer as a sort of Scarlet Pimpernel figure—'Is he in heaven? Is he in hell?'

Charter went in search of Finn, expecting to find that he had checked out, but he had gone for a walk and would be back for lunch. By then the Press would probably be arriving in force. It looked as if he would be handing a real can of worms to the local constabulary. On the other hand the presence of the Press might prove daunting to the hoaxer, too.

And, sure enough, looking out of the window, he saw the first of several men and women of the Press and two photographers arguing with Andrew Tierney on the front step of the hotel. He ran downstairs to bring his authority to bear, too late to stop Andrew from trying to sock one of them on the jaw but in time to save the man's camera from being flung down the steps.

'Don't be a fool,' he said under his breath. 'Can't you see that this gives them a much better story? To be continued in tomorrow's paper and then on, *ad infinitum*?'

'They've already done as much as it takes to ruin us, and thank you very much for that.'

The journalists then tried to inveigle Charter into giving an impromptu Press conference on the hotel steps.

'No,' he said, 'I've nothing to say. Go and have breakfast.'

They went away to raid the Buttery. As he turned to go back into the hotel he saw Corinna watching him indignantly from the door to the kitchens. It was irritating that he couldn't go over to explain to her that he had been stalling the Press. She swung on her heel and went back into the kitchens.

A heart-stopping screaming began somewhere in the hotel. It soared to a high note and held it, ululating, deafening, terrifying. Charter raced for the staircase followed by Andrew, and Corinna and her staff came hurtling out of the kitchens. Emmie Pomfret was on her knees on the landing shaking her head from side to side as she screamed. Charter slapped her sharply across the face then took both her hands in his. Her eyes opened even wider and then relaxed as she turned to him, sobbing harshly. He went down on his knees beside her.

'What is it, Mrs Pomfret? What's the matter?'

She shook her head helplessly.

'I must know what's wrong. Has something frightened you?'

She pointed behind her into the room from which she had come, stabbing the air jerkily, her mouth working, her face moist and white as paper.

'It's him! It's Michael. He's not there. He hasn't been there all night. And there's blood on the duvet, his blood on the duvet. The connecting door's still locked. It's been locked all night!'

She covered her face with her hands and collapsed ungracefully on the carpet. Then Corinna was putting an arm round her.

Charter went into the bedroom. He stood just inside the door. The professor had not slept in his bed, unless someone had remade the bed in order to give just this impression. The room was tidy except for a table near the window which was covered with books and papers. He went closer to the bed and saw what had frightened Emmie. The light-coloured duvet was heavily stained and the stains were dark red.

Touching nothing he went out on to the landing. Corinna was leading Emmie towards the open door of another room beyond the bedroom.

'Where are you going?' he asked.

'Mrs Pomfret sleeps in her own bedroom beyond the sitting-room. I'm taking her to lie down.'

'No. Do you mind? You must find her another room. I'll have to seal off this set of rooms until the police get here.'

Her eyes flew up to his, wide and startled. 'Police?'

'I'm afraid so.'

'I'll take her to my room then. For once we're full up.'

'And I'll need the keys to their rooms.'

'I'll tell the housekeeper,' she said and Andrew appeared and helped her to lead Emmie away.

Charter leaned over the bannisters below which a number of the staff and guests had congregated.

'Please go back to the dining-room,' he said. 'We'll let you know what's going on as soon as we can.'

Having locked up the rooms he went back to his own and telephoned Sherwood Lodge. He was put through to Detective Superintendent Philip Nolan and introduced himself as Detective Chief Superintendent John Charter of Penfoldshire Constabulary.

'I intended to come over and see you later,' he said, 'but now we've got a missing person, possibly murder or kidnapping. A visiting American professor.'

The matter-of-fact Nottinghamshire voice showed no surprise. 'Right,' he said. 'Five minutes.' And in five minutes he was there, only to be superseded a few minutes later by the arrival of Detective Chief Superintendent Robert Falkner, who at once assumed the mantle of Senior Investigating Officer.

Charter hurriedly explained to this short, middle-aged police officer with a calm manner but chilly and searching blue eyes.

'I've no intention,' he said, 'of getting under your feet in your manor. I simply happen to be here attending the conference. I came for a specific ulterior purpose and in following that up I've gleaned a good deal of information you'll want to have. When you've inspected the scene you may want to have a talk. Here are the keys to the professor's rooms.'

'Thank you. We'll get on then.' The tone was non-committal.

'Just one thing. Before you do anything else it would be a good idea to send a man over to the fort on the other side of the Upper Lake and cordon off a bit of land behind it where someone made a bonfire in the small hours last night. The lab may want to look at anything you find there.'

'Right. I'll do that.'

They went upstairs and Charter went to find Corinna.

'Look my dear,' he said, 'I need a private room for talking to the superintendent.'

'You can use the office through the kitchen,' she said.

'Thank you.'

'Do you think he's dead?' she asked fearfully.

'There's no point in speculating.'

'It'll finish us,' she said. 'Just as things were beginning to go so well. He's dead. I'm sure of it. We're done for.'

Charter looked at her for a long moment of disillusion.

'I hope not,' he said politely. 'I'll send the staff in.' And he went out into the hall, summoned the housekeeper and the girls who were still gathered there and sent them to the kitchens. Then he went outside and watched the RPS members walking across to the crypt where the morning's lectures were to be held. The Orangery was locked. They all looked chastened and he felt sorry for Martin who had planned the conference so carefully. He turned back to the hotel garden and found a bench where he could sit and watch what was going on.

Fresh scents came from the dazzling white blooms of old roses. Sunlight filtered through transparent young foliage. From across the

106

fields the woods, the quarry and the Lower Lake came the faint but clear sound of church bells from St Mary Magdalene at Hucknall a mile and a half away.

Soon all peacefulness was at an end. A succession of police cars and vans arrived in front of the Abbey, disgorging uniformed and CID men, scene-of-crime men, underwater search teams, dogs and dog handlers, all sorts of specialists and equipment.

From his bench in the garden Charter could watch all this and admire the dispatch with which his Nottinghamshire colleagues got to work.

And there he was found a quarter of an hour later by the young PC he had talked to outside the Abbey early that morning.

'Sir,' he said, 'the chief superintendent has asked me to tell you that we've found the professor.'

Charter looked at him and something in his expression made the young man say, 'I'm sorry, sir. He's drowned. In the Slype. The superintendent says he'll come and see you as soon as he can. Oh, and the professor hasn't got a stitch on him.'

'Very well,' said Charter. 'I'll wait here. Thank you. You'd better get back over there.'

The young man went and Charter sat for a long time plunged in thought.

This was now a case that the Nottinghamshire Police would treat as high priority and one that he would give a lot to be able to take on himself.

CHAPTER FIFTEEN

I love to lose myself in a mystery.
SIR THOMAS BROWNE

Who on earth would want to kill Professor Pomfret? If indeed, he had been killed. He racked his brains and could think of no sensible motive for a murder except the professor's wealth and how could that fit in with the series of hoaxes? Having no firm information about how he met his death he could not usefully begin to theorize about that. But all sorts of ideas came to the fore about the nakedness of the victim.

Charter absolutely ruled out the possibility that the man slept in the buff. He was quite sure that Pomfret had with him a plethora of pyjamas in finest sea island cotton. What was being burned last night? And by whom? Was it the hoaxer or was it the murderer? Or were they one and the same? Had the murderer made the bonfire in order to burn Professor Pomfret's clothes? The bloodstains in the bedroom indicated that the killer's clothes would be covered with bloodstains. The man probably knew the lab might find traces of fibre from the

108

professor's clothes attached to his own. So he stripped the body before putting it into the Slype and then burned the clothes on the bonfire. He probably made assurance doubly sure by burning his own too. So if he took incriminating bloodstains and fibres away from the bedroom they would safely go up in smoke.

Did he know that putting the body into the cold waters of the Slype would make the computation of the time of death immeasurably more difficult for the lab? It almost seemed as if the man was a policeman. He knew too much. On the other hand he might have had quite different motives for doing these things.

It seemed likely that the man who hit Charter over the head on the shore of the lake was the man who killed the professor. But what was he doing over there when he must have expected Emmie to find her husband gone when she went back to the hotel at 1 a.m.? If she had then raised the alarm the man would be in great danger of being discovered beside his bonfire. Had he failed to anticipate this or did he know that Emmie slept alone and had quarrelled with her husband, so would be unlikely to find her husband gone until she got up in the morning?

Why make the bonfire so near to the Abbey? It would have been much safer to drive off somewhere with the clothes (and also whatever he burned that was made of paper) in plastic bags. Unless he was someone at the hotel with a room to get back to before morning, or perhaps even a shared room and a partner who might wake up and find him gone and later, when the news of the murder broke, develop suspicions. And then it might also be someone who couldn't go further afield because he hadn't come in a car. Emmie?

Not Emmie. She couldn't possibly have hit Charter and tied him up, or dragged her husband over to the Slype. Or could she? Surely Emmie had never heard of a quick release knot. But how could he tell? She had once been young and agile. Perhaps she was a yachtswoman. Perhaps a horsewoman. Emmie had a good motive. Huge wealth and the freedom to do with it whatever she wished. Who would want to kill the professor for any other reason? The wealth must come into it. No, not must. But very likely did.

Martin might claim that academic rivalries were strong enough to cause animosity enough to spark off the hoaxes but would he claim that such rivalries could spark off murder?

Who, apart from Emmie, stood to gain from the professor's death? In view of the exhibition she had put on last night she must be an obvious suspect as far as motive went. But Emmie couldn't personally have managed the hoaxes. In theory she could have hired someone else to do them but she knew nothing

110

about the society. She told everyone it was the first time she had accompanied her husband to a conference. So how would she have known what sort of hoax would be appropriate?

That the hoaxes came into it Charter was certain. The possibility might even arise that the death of the professor was a hoax gone wrong, in which case Charter, who had been asked to protect the society from the hoaxer, had let the side down badly. Memo: was the bonfire a hoax? Could it be possible that the man who had lit the bonfire was the hoaxer and that the murder had nothing to do with him? Charter thought not.

What sort of hoax could end with the professor dead? Or was the death the aim? Were the hoaxes a smokescreen intended to camouflage murder? That couldn't be ruled out. If the death was the aim and the professor's money the goal then the hoaxes were a very lucrative plan and well worth all the long-term planning that had gone into them.

It was now clear that more investigation must be done into the three London hoaxes: Martin's flat, the London Library and the Royal Institution. Perhaps his task should be to get up to the London Library at once. There was, it seemed to him, an outside chance that a proper investigation at the Library might, even after all these months, produce the identity of the hoaxer, or at least of some accomplice.

He must be either a member of the society or someone connected with it so closely as to know its members, and to have access to its office in the Frost Building. Could the professor have hired someone to do the hoaxes and done one on himself to hide his tracks? And could the fact that he was the hoaxer have led to his death?

He was, as usual, going too fast and theorizing way ahead of the evidence. He would do well to remember that he was a policeman not a psychiatrist, a novelist or an Hercule Poirot.

Falkner came across the garden and he got up and went to meet him.

'I'm going to see Mrs Pomfret,' Falkner said. 'And then I'd like to have that talk. Is that all right by you?'

'Of course,' said Charter.

Ten minutes later Charter took Falkner through to the office beyond the kitchen. Preparations for lunch were well in hand and Corinna came over to greet the superintendent and said, 'We usually do salads and soups for lunch. Shall I send some in for you? Or sandwiches? And wine or beer?'

'That's very kind,' said Falkner, 'but I'll lunch later. We do provide mobile food on jobs like this. It's quicker and we won't have to put you to any trouble.' His eyes softened as he looked at her. Charter realized for the first time that Corinna only had to appear looking

112

slightly harassed and everybody smiled and began to look after her.

They sat on either side of a large desk, its scuffed leather top covered with out-trays and in-trays. A WPC stood outside the door.

'The first problem is that we've got to get on fast,' Falkner told him. 'This lot are stopping here for two more days and nights and then they'll want to be off in all directions. I doubt if we can detain fifty members of this conference without a shred of evidence.'

'Some may have left already,' said Charter.

'Yes. A Professor Kristeller left this morning for the States before all this happened. He must have know we'd want to interview everybody about that extraordinary affair last night. Incidentally, that's two professors down. I hope he did, in fact, leave. I don't want to find more than one murdered academic. Then there's a Mrs Lavinia Wallace who informs us she has to spend the day in London tomorrow. She works for Matthew Frost and it seems he's a hard taskmaster. I'm having a DI take her statement this afternoon.

'Now we think that the man didn't drown. It looks as if he was knocked down in his room, hit his head and probably died there. He has a head wound. We don't know whether he was wearing day clothes or pyjamas at the time because he was naked when we found him. As soon as Mrs Pomfret feels up to it we'll get her to check his clothes to see if anything is missing. There's no evidence that he was in the bath. There are no discarded clothes lying about. I don't believe a man of that age would be sleeping naked. It wasn't all that warm last night. The murderer may have disposed of the clothes because his own were likely to be contaminated by them.'

'So he has probably disposed of his own too.'

'Quite likely. The biggest problem is that icy-cold tap water in the Slype. It's a big complication for the lab and there's no evidence yet as to time. Mrs Pomfret says she didn't go to the professor's room when she went back to the hotel last night because it was very late and they'd had a row because he refused to escort her to the dinner. So in theory he could have been murdered at any time after she left the room to go to the dinner at about eight o'clock.'

'Someone lit a bonfire at about three o'clock last night behind the fort on the other side of the lake. He thought it would be hidden from sight over there but I spotted it and swam over to investigate.'

'Swam?'

'Quickest way. He might have been long gone if I'd gone round the lake. I could hear the bloke stamping out the fire but he saw me or heard me and crept up on me and when I came round I was tied to a tree by my wrists. Oddest thing of all—he'd tied me with a quick release knot so it didn't take me long to get free.'

'Sounds like the sort of thing a woman might do. If she could tie the knot.'

Charter gave him an ironic look. 'You have to be careful not to say that sort of thing among this crowd.'

'You didn't see him?'

'No. But I did collect some debris from the fire. There's evidence that he burned what looks to me like papers but the lab will pronounce on that. What I found is waiting for them in a plastic bag.'

'You suspected murder then?'

'No. But the hoaxer was beginning to worry me. And, of course, my mind turned to possible theft from the collection here.'

'Why would he burn what he'd stolen?'

'Only if he'd done something that he felt would alert us and so he decided to abort the whole thing. He wouldn't want to be found with anything incriminating and if he was a member of the conference he couldn't very well leave early without arousing suspicion.'

'This Professor Kristeller did leave early. And left the country into the bargain.'

'True. I expect you'll chase him up. It occurred to me last night that the man was burning some loot because he'd been detected and perhaps had had to fight his way out. If he hurt someone badly he might panic and destroy whatever he'd stolen. I went over to check with your PC that all was well in the

Abbey and he'd spoken to the security men so I assumed my theory was wrong.'

'Well how does this bomb scare we were called in for last night fit in with all this?'

'I'll have to go back a fairly long way to throw light on that.'

'Do that.'

Charter told him and the superintendent looked at him in amazement as the story unfolded.

'So they called you in to protect them from a hoaxer?'

'Yes. Unofficially. I'm on leave. And I haven't done a very good job for them. It was only with the bomb scare last night that I decided to call in the Force this morning. If I'd known, of course, I'd have done it last night and sealed off the bonfire. But until now it's all been rather tenuous. The boat bomb could have been nothing to do with the society and been just a coincidence. So could the burglary in London. The London Library incident and the false invitation to the distinguished scholar were relatively harmless. But the bomb scare last night was mischievous. This hoaxer is coming over to me now as a dangerous man. I'm convinced now that he did organize the bomb in the boat in Venice. If I'd seriously suspected murder I'd have got in touch with you at once.

'The question now being are the hoaxer, the maker of the bonfire and the murderer one and the same?'

'Suppose the charred papers show that he did steal something at the hotel, not the Abbey, and the professor surprised him. In which case the professor, not a security man got bashed by accident in the course of some offence.'

'Professor Pomfret was mega-rich. There may be a safe in the hotel bedroom.'

'The wife will know what he had with him. But if this scenario is not the right one she'd be my prime suspect. She presumably inherits and she may be quite strong even though she looks such a skinny little woman.'

'If she did it, and I don't think she could have done it without an accomplice, then the hoaxer and the bonfire are out of it.'

'We'll keep an open mind on that. She had a row with him last night. Three separate people have told us that already. And she told him she wished she could go on a widows' cruise.'

'People say that sort of thing to their husbands. Fortunately they don't usually follow it up by knocking him down and drowning him.'

'No doubt we'll know more when we've got on a bit with the statements. I'm rather sorry it's happened here. It's our great showpiece and we don't like people fooling about with it.'

'I feel responsible in an illogical sort of way. I don't want to get in your way but if I can help I'd like to.'

'If you can hang about I'd be grateful.'

'What about my heading for London tomorrow to check up on the London hoaxes? Now the man has been murdered the incident at the London Library will need proper investigation which I'm sure it didn't get from these people.'

'Good. That'll help with the manpower on the ground here. Perhaps you could deal with the American lawyer too. He's in England at a legal get-together in London. A routine check on the will.'

'Right. I'll do that.'

'Then I'll get on with some more of the preliminary interviews and we'll have another talk later. Good thing we've got the tape recorder from last night's incident but it's a pity he got away with the tape. If we once got a voice print we'd have your hoaxer on toast.'

CHAPTER SIXTEEN

In London! What would you do there?

SWIFT

At eleven o'clock on Monday morning Charter walked into the St James's Square garden past the mulberry tree and the statue of William of Orange sitting on his magnificent bronze horse in his mock Roman armour under the plane trees, and came out into the Square facing the

East India Club with its white façade, the frieze picked out in blue, and the row of gas flambeaux along the railings at the front. He crossed over and went up past the Clerical and Medical building and in at the front door of the modest house near the corner which houses the London Library.

The staff of the Library were only too willing to help him. One of them took him upstairs to the literature book-stacks on the second floor and they walked along one of the narrow passages between the stacks to where, under the tall windows which spanned the wall length on the St James's Square front, a narrow wooden table and a straight-backed chair stood.

'That's where he sat that day,' said Mr Mablethorpe.

'I suppose it's quieter up here than in the reading room.'

'No, I wouldn't say that. People come up to look along the stacks for books. And the porters bring books up in the lift.'

'The lift? May I see it?'

They went back towards the door and examined the old-fashioned dumb waiter.

'The porters don't put the books back,' explained Mr Mablethorpe. 'Members of the staff come up to put them in their places in the stacks.'

'Could anyone get into the lift and come up without being seen?'

'Much easier and quieter to come up the stairs.'

'Could anyone come in and up to this room without coming to the front desk?'

'Yes, he could. We couldn't possibly be sure we'd notice everyone who came in. If he wasn't returning or taking out books and just wanted to consult books on the shelves or look up a reference he wouldn't need to come to the desk.'

'Can you give me a list of the members who did announce themselves that day, as well as a full list of all the members?'

'Including the corporate members?'

'Yes, please.'

As they walked downstairs again Mr Mablethorpe said, 'There is one way you could get in here without coming through the front door, though you'd still have to come through the main hall. Normally the service door in Duke Street is closed but last September we had workmen in. Someone might have slipped in then without being noticed.'

'It must have been a member who knew the layout.'

'We do have Reading Room membership on a temporary basis for people who don't want to take books out. It's not renewable but it would give someone with his wits about him the chance to familiarize himself with the set-up here. I'll give you a list of the people with Reading Room membership around that time.'

'Thank you. Does corporate membership mean that everyone in the firm has access here?'

'No. Only one person comes to fetch the books for use on their own premises.'

'I see.'

'We were all very shocked at what happened. But it's difficult to see how we could have prevented it. All the man needed was a bottle of red ink. You don't expect a crazy act like that. I'm afraid any member of the staff could have smuggled in the red ink and waited till the professor had gone out to lunch.'

'I'm sure none of you did. We'll try to make sure there's no bad publicity for the Library.'

Mr Mablethorpe smiled as he shook hands. 'We'll survive a little bad publicity. Here is the list of members.'

Having studied this, Charter went out into the Square. He strolled along to Duke Street and on past the Bonbonnière with its bright red canopy and into the Red Lion, an elaborate old-fashioned London pub with frosted glass and dark mahogany and gaslight globes adapted for electricity.

Lavinia Wallace was sitting on a high bar stool, her chin propped on an elegant wrist and her hair falling forward to hide her face.

When she saw him she stepped down gracefully and motioned him to follow her to a compartment where they could be relatively private.

'I'm busy today,' she said coolly. 'I would have talked to you willingly yesterday at Nottingham but today I left early to get to London before rush hour so that I could get to the office in good time and I simply haven't got time to spare. I've already given the Nottingham police a statement. I can't imagine why you insisted on meeting me here.'

There was a certain speculation in her eyes as she looked at him and he realized that it had crossed her mind that he admired her and had arranged the meeting for that reason.

'May I order something for you?' he asked.

'A glass of white wine and a smoked salmon sandwich.'

He ordered the same for himself, then said to her firmly, 'I find that the Frost Company has corporate membership of the London Library. I need to know whether you or any other member of the staff at the Frost building visited the London Library on the day Professor Pomfret's paper was damaged with red ink.'

She looked at him without expression. 'I can't answer for anyone else,' she said. 'I know I didn't.'

'How do you know that, Mrs Wallace? Do you remember the date?'

'Of course. I arrange the programme of speakers.'

'Does Mr Frost use the Library often?'

'It depends on what he's doing.'

'So he hasn't been working there lately?'

'No. He's been away a lot.'

'I see. Did Mr Frost have business dealings with Professor Pomfret?'

She was thinking hard. He got the impression that she was trying to make up her mind between more than one possible answer.

'No,' she said. 'Not apart from RPS. They are both on the International Council so they sometimes have to talk to each other about matters to do with the society.'

'So would they meet when the professor came to England?'

Again she paused. 'Sometimes they would.'

'Did Mr Frost invite him home?'

'I believe he did once but Mrs Frost isn't interested in Mr Frost's literary friends.'

'So she doesn't accompany him to conferences?'

'Never. She stops up there at Gonalston with her garden and her horses.' A contemptuous tone came into her voice and Charter looked at her until her eyes fell.

'Can you tell me anything about Mr Frost's daughter and her husband?' he asked. 'It seemed to me that Mrs Tierney has to work extremely hard.'

'Yes. She often looks worn out. Andrew is bone idle. He's supposed to handle reception and entertaining and accounts. In practice I'm pretty sure she does everything.'

'Matthew Frost can't be too pleased about that. I would have thought he could have afforded to provide more staff for his daughter.'

She looked at him pityingly. 'He's a businessman, Mr Charter. You can't expect him to behave like a fairy godmother. If he helped Corinna he'd be making a gift to Andrew and that wouldn't suit him at all. And besides, even quite prosperous businessmen are often stretched to the limit financially. They can't take on new commitments without selling shares or cutting down in other directions. He wouldn't want to do that, however fond he may be of his daughter. You ought to know that successful businessmen care more for balance sheets than people.'

'Has that been your experience with Mr Frost too?'

Again she thought for a moment before she spoke.

'More or less,' she said, consideringly. 'They don't make exceptions to that rule—the rule of putting the balance sheet first.'

'And have you any idea who could have suppressed the letter from Bracousse accepting the invitation from RPS to speak at the Royal Institution?'

'No such letter arrived.'

'And who could have stolen the writing paper with the RPS letterhead?'

'More or less anyone who entered our office.

124

There would always be sheets of paper lying around. As for the letter of acceptance, the writer would surely give him the wrong address to make sure of getting no reply.'

'I think he would if he had his wits about him. And I'm beginning to think this gentleman has all his wits about him. Or, of course, this lady. There's nothing to indicate that this couldn't have been done by a woman.'

She stared at him coolly.

'Is that all?'

He stood up. 'Yes, Mrs Wallace. Thank you for your help. I may have to talk to you again. Do you plan to come back to Nottingham?'

'Yes.'

Before driving back to Norman Abbey, Charter made his way over to Westminster and joined the Pomfrets' attorney in the foyer of St Ermin's Hotel with its elaborate plasterwork ceilings, its galleries and balustrades, its potted plants and its great chandeliers. They lay back in deep armchairs and waiters brought them tea and cucumber sandwiches. A pretty girl played the harp in the gallery. A few people wandered from time to time across the thick pile of the pastel-coloured carpets. It was old-fashioned and reassuring until one noticed a party of agitated Japanese businessmen arguing over their itinerary near the doors.

Stephen Cook was dressed as impeccably as Professor Pomfret but gave a different impression as he was short, broad, overweight and slightly rumpled.

'This is a horrible thing,' he said. 'How is Mrs Pomfret?'

'Reasonably under control, I'm told,' said Charter. 'I haven't seen her since the body was found. Detective Chief Superintendent Falkner, the Senior Investigating Officer, has asked me to have a word with you about the will. Mrs Pomfret told us you were arriving in London yesterday.'

'That's right. I'll be happy to help in any way that I properly can.'

'Can you give us the gist of the will?'

He put the tips of his fingers together and hesitated, then said, 'I don't see why not. Emmie's going to have to know sometime. He changed his will three years ago. She had insisted that everything was to go to her and that it was up to her to decide what to give to Virginia and Milton. He willed it all to her. Then he had second thoughts. Emmie is a very autocratic woman. I think he thought she might hang on to the lot and use it to make the children toe the line. So he divided it in three, a third to her and a third to each of the children.'

'Did she know this?'

'I think it's highly unlikely. I doubt if he would dare to tell her and I don't blame him. She would have been very angry.'

'Then,' Charter said, 'as far as she knew, his death would have brought her a great deal of money and with it supreme power over her children.'

'Well, I suppose that's right. But Emmie wouldn't have murdered Michael. Not murder.'

'Do you think she might have suspected that he had changed his will?'

'No. I'm sure it never entered her head. She had him pretty well under control. She knew her own power over him and she used it without scruple. But, underneath it all, I'm quite sure that she loved him.'

'Any other relevant bequests?'

'None at all.'

'Thank you then. That's all I need for the moment. Can we have this all officially from your firm as soon as possible?'

'I'll get it all dug out and sent to you.'

*   *   *

Charter went out into Caxton Street in search of a cab.

Arriving back at the Abbey he met Martin coming out of the North of Trent.

'Ah,' said Martin, 'just the man I've been looking for. What's going on?'

'A very thorough and efficient police investigation. You'd be surprised at how much ground they'll already have covered.'

Martin looked momentarily apprehensive and Charter thought, he looks exactly as a murderer might look on hearing that the police

127

are getting warm.

'I need to make an announcement about when they can go home. What's happened? We heard a rumour that the professor was found drowned in the Slype. We can't keep all these people cooped up here you know. Not for much longer. Several of the academics have important engagements.'

'I'll ask Falkner to come over and talk to them all first thing in the morning.'

'The superintendent? Not you?'

'It's his job, Martin. I can't barge in on this one.'

'Was it the hoaxer?'

'It's no use speculating about it. We don't know.'

'It's hard not to speculate in the circumstances. After all, we're all shut up here with a murderer.'

'I doubt if this murderer will murder again. The place is overrun with PCs. It would be very rash to try anything more.'

'Haven't we the evidence of our eyes that this is a very rash murderer?'

'Well, yes. I'm sorry by the way about the publicity yesterday morning though it was bound to happen after the murder. But it was a pity it hit the Sunday papers. You should never have had Finn.'

'He wrote quite a reasonable piece on the Venice conference. It never occurred to me that he'd do what he did yesterday morning.'

'Once there's murder you're fair game for them I'm afraid.'

'I give up. It's all over with us. We might as well cut our losses and halt the drive for new members. Who's going to want to join a society at whose conference eminent professors get murdered and people are marooned over the remains of their dinner on account of a bomb scare?'

'Nonsense. You'll be inundated. They'll all pour in agog for the excitement and the publicity.'

CHAPTER SEVENTEEN

By vilest means pursues the vilest ends,
Fawns in the day and Butchers in the
night.

CRABBE

Charter went to find Falkner. They asked Corinna's permission to use the office and she came with them.

'Coffee?' she asked, with the practised smile of the efficient hostess and went out of the room. A few minutes later the housekeeper came in with coffee and Bath Olivers. Charter was not forgiven.

Falkner was brisk and smiling. 'Any progress in London?' he asked, and Charter told him.

'No one officially in the Library on the day in September when Professor Pomfret's papers were destroyed seems to have any connection with the list of participants in the conference here but we'll need to do a lot more hard work on that. The Frost organization has corporate membership but no one remembers seeing him in the Library that day. Lavinia Wallace, who usually takes the books out claims she wasn't there either.'

'Well, we've made some progress here while you've been away. He died hitting his head on the bed post after someone knocked him out in his bedroom. They can't make a decent shot at the time because of the cooling of the body in the Slype. He'd been in the water a considerable time.'

'That presents us with a problem.'

'Yes. When did he get the body over to the Slype? He couldn't have done it after Emmie went back to her room because the alarm system was turned on again by then and the doors were all locked.'

'The windows too.'

'Right. When could he do it? The professor was still alive when Mrs Pomfret left the room to go across to the Abbey—if we are to believe Mrs Pomfret. All the guests at the Abbey went upstairs at eight-thirty for the reception which went on for an hour and a half. It seems to me that the only time he'd stand a chance of getting the body over there would be after they were all safely upstairs and before all the activity started downstairs for serving the dinner at ten. That means he must have been killed between eight and nine and carted over there at about nine-fifteen or so.'

'No one would have the nerve to carry a naked body about the place in those circumstances.'

'You'd think not, wouldn't you? But we've got some evidence of how he did it. It was still risky but it worked. One of the gardeners found a wheelbarrow standing near the entrance to the garden beside the Priory ruin on Sunday morning. And in the cloister-garth we found some gardening tools, an empty refuse sack with bloodstains on the inside, a pair of dungarees and a cap from the garden shed. This character put on the dungarees over his glad rags, pulled the hat down over his eyes, stuffed the body into the sack and wheeled it over to the Abbey. He carried the sack and the tools into the cloister and laid them down in a corner to look as if one of the gardeners had been interrupted in his work and would be back to finish it in the morning. That's where the body lay throughout the reception and the dinner.'

'I see,' said Charter thoughtfully. 'So he wasn't carrying a naked body openly into the cloisters. If someone had seen him he might easily have got away with being seen as one of the gardeners dumping a bag of peat in the cloister-garth for spreading around at a later stage.'

'That's right. And Pomfret was a very small, frail man so the sack wouldn't be too heavy.'

'He must have done it between half past eight and nine.'

'How do you make that out?'

'Because that was the time set for the arrival of the local mayor. Everyone at the conference, including Corinna and her staff, were under instructions to be upstairs in the Great Hall for the reception and the speeches. The killer knew he'd be unlikely to find anyone about downstairs between eight-thirty and nine. The security people would be concentrating on the galleries upstairs. I went up with the mayor's party and there wasn't a soul about downstairs at that time.'

'I'll check whether there was anyone on the door. I reckon there must have been.'

'One man who was patrolling up and down. What would he see? One of the gardeners heading for the cloister-garth with a sack. I'd like to bet they use students and other casual labour who'd be working at weekends and in the evenings.'

'You'd win your bet. They do.'

'And if he'd seen anything suspicious the doorman would have said so by now.'

'If this is right the man kept his head in horrendous circumstances. He must have gone into the Pomfret room thinking they'd both gone over to the reception, found Pomfret there, hit him, and decided to dump the body when he saw what he'd done.'

'And the body in the sack lay with the gardening tools in the cloister-garth till after the dinner while he walked up to the reception.'

'And if we're lucky someone may have seen him going upstairs after the mayor's arrival.'

'Unless he lurked somewhere until after the speeches and mingled with the crowd coming down.'

'If this is right you realize that it lets out all the people who were prominent at the reception for the mayor.'

'It lets them out on the act of killing the professor but not of being instigator of the murder. Any of them could have used an accomplice. And some could have slipped away. The hall was crammed with people—all the members of the conference plus the mayor's party and all sorts of local people invited for the reception but not the dinner. It wouldn't be easy to spot the absence of any one person unless you were actually searching for him.'

'Presumably Martin Proctor was involved in the speeches.'

'Yes. And the Hellvellyns and the Wallaces were in the reception line but most of them moved away long before the mayor arrived. So I'm afraid we can only rule out Martin at this stage.'

'Well, in time we may pinpoint the movements of the others—if anyone saw them, remembered seeing them and happened to look at his watch at the time. It's heart-breaking. Now let's go on to the next thing: when did he put the body in the Slype?'

'Not before the dinner because we all looked into the Slype on our way to the Orangery to admire the effect made by filling the sunken passageway with water.'

'The fact is, he didn't need to put the body in the Slype at all. He could have left it to be discovered by the gardeners in the cloister-garth next day. I reckon he saw his chance. After the dinner and before the place was locked up again.'

'But your lads were here by then.'

'Yes but he knew that they'd finished searching by the time everyone was allowed to leave. He knew they hadn't found the body in the cloister-garth (and I'll have something to say to my lads about that). So as everyone walks round the cloisters and through the crypt to the front entrance he hangs back, perhaps hides in the dark part of the cloisters where there are no flares because nobody is going that way. When the last foot disappears round the corner he dashes to the cloister-garth, puts on the gloves (he must have worn gloves but he isn't stupid—he didn't leave them for us) takes the sack to the Slype, tips the body into the water, shuts the door tight, whips back into the garth and leaves everything in a neat pile. The whole thing takes two minutes. He doesn't need the disguise this time. He then dashes for the door and mingles with the crowd. It would take that old lady much longer to walk to the door from the Orangery than for our man to dump the body and catch up. Man or woman I should have said.'

'Man or woman?'

'Why not? He was small and thin. I reckon Mrs Pomfret could have done it herself.'

'Seriously?'

'Seriously. She's my prime suspect. With an accomplice perhaps.'

Charter got up. 'This looks like going on for several hours. Bitter, Falkner?'

'Lager, Charter.'

'John, as a matter of fact.'

'And Robert.'

CHAPTER EIGHTEEN

But die, and she'll adore you.

POPE

Charter said, 'I can't agree with you on Emmie Pomfret. She had the motive but I can't see her doing the deed. She does stand to inherit a lot of money, though not as much as she expected.

He changed his will three years ago. She only gets a third.'

'But she didn't know it? And if she did find out, she would be very angry. So that might be an even better motive. We all know she has an uncontrolled temper. I find it odd and distinctly suspicious that she opened the door and had that row with her husband out on the landing. Most people would shut the door of the room and abuse their old man in decent privacy. But what does she do? She flings the door open and yells at him at the top of her voice. Perhaps she yelled at him to give everyone within earshot the idea that he was still alive. Perhaps she'd already killed him by then.'

'She went straight over to the Abbey. There's no way she could have crept back to collect the body.'

'No. My theory requires that she planned this well in advance and hired some sort of help. The hit man would have been in the room when she started screaming at the husband and he would move the body.'

'Is this pure speculation or a serious theory?'

Falkner smiled. 'Pure speculation. But there is something else that points to Emmie Pomfret. She's been trying to muddy the waters: to make us think it was robbery.'

'To be fair to the woman we have already entertained the idea that that's what it was.'

'Yes. That's what it may have been. But

there isn't another suspect with the faintest motive for killing the man. In any case let's get her out of the way.'

'Right. How did she muddy the waters?'

'She told me something was missing. He had a briefcase with him filled with Swiss francs. I asked her what it was for and she got quite angry. Said he didn't talk to her about his business affairs.'

'Then how did she know the case was full of money?'

'She opened it of course. But she's not going to admit it.'

'I don't believe she could be the hoaxer. And all this leaping about in the middle of the night and making of bonfires and dumping bodies in theatrical places fits in exactly with the sort of mind that planned the hoaxes. He could have pitched the body into the lake instead of taking it over to the Slype. It would have been just as difficult for the lab and much less dangerous for him.'

'I'm not sure it would have been all that less dangerous. He couldn't be sure no one was left in the hotel. Think of all those windows upstairs and downstairs looking out on the lakeside. And all the outside lights were switched on. If anyone had seen him out in the open he'd have been sunk. At least in the cloisters and crypt he could check that there was no one around. And the cloisters are glassed in so you can't see across them unless you press your nose against the glass. I reckon I'd rather have done what he did than risk being seen tipping a body into the lake.'

'This briefcase full of money. He did have a briefcase on him when I drove him to Southwell just before midday on Saturday. I'd like to go and ask her about it. Shall I?'

'Now? It's a bit late isn't it?'

'May I borrow a WPC?'

'Yes, you may. And while you're about it ask her about a mythical package she also mentioned.'

'There was a package. He went off to the bank to collect some sterling he'd arranged for and when he came back he was carrying this package.'

'So it did exist? It seemed to me that the package was gilding the lily. The briefcase was quite enough for a reasonable red herring. She said he dropped the briefcase and the package in their room on his way to the lecture. The thing is, there's no sign of a package. The briefcase is still there but she claims that the money has disappeared.'

'I'll see what I can get out of her.'

'If you say the package did exist outside her imagination that changes things. There are some interesting possibilities.'

*   *   *

Emmie opened the door of her room in a velvet

dressing-gown, her hair wrapped up in a silk turban. She motioned Charter and the WPC to sit down.

'I'm sorry it's so late,' Charter said, 'but we want to sort this out as fast as we can. You told Mr Falkner that last Saturday afternoon your husband brought a package with him from Southwell. We need to know what was in that package. He may have told you. If not it would be very natural behaviour on your part if you opened the package to verify the contents. Did you?'

'Did I what?' She looked at him uncertainly.

He smiled at her reassuringly. 'Did you peek, Mrs Pomfret?'

'Well, yes,' she said reluctantly, 'as a matter of fact I did think I ought to—er—verify the contents.'

'And what did you find?'

'Nothing but an old manuscript.'

'You don't know what it was? Did you notice a name, a place, a printer? Or a publisher?'

'No. It was in handwriting. In ink—old-fashioned. The sort of thing that thrilled Michael.'

'And you've no idea what it was? A novel? A poem?'

'It was a story I think—a sort of reminiscence. There was a lot about Aberdeen at the beginning and I do remember the name Scrope later on. I remember that because I

139

never know whether to pronounce it Scroop or Scrope. But it was very difficult to read in that old script so I put it back.'

'That's enough to be going on with,' said Charter in a startled voice, and he wrenched his mind away from the possibilities this opened up.

'And it was then that you found all the money in the briefcase?'

'Oh no,' she said. 'It was then that I found all the money had gone.'

'Then it was earlier in the morning that you saw the money in the briefcase?'

'No. I saw it there the day before. Do you think that's why he was killed?'

'I can't say, Mrs Pomfret. But we're going to find out. One more question: the local police asked me to go and see your attorney, Mr Cook, yesterday. I expect you knew he was in London for a legal conference. Had you seen your husband's will?'

'I don't need to see it. Michael and I left everything to each other.'

'I'm afraid that isn't so. It seems that your husband changed his will three years ago and divided his estate equally between you and each of your two children. A third to each.'

'What!' She looked astonished. 'Only a third to me!' And then she surprised him. A look almost of admiration came over her face. 'Well, who would have thought he would do that?'

'It's disappointing for you of course.'

'Disappointing? I won't even notice the difference. But I ought to be very angry with him and heaven knows why I'm not. He did it to make the children free of me. He didn't want them to have to come to me for money. Well, he's freed them, but he's freed me too. I can do exactly as I like now.'

'Which you couldn't do while your husband was alive?'

'What are you saying? Of course I could! I could do exactly as I liked, and what's more I had someone to do it with. So don't talk like that. What use is it to be free without your partner?' She began to cry harshly.

He stood up, 'Shall I fetch someone to you?'

She shook her head. 'No, I'm all right. It's just that I'm going to miss the old thing. Go on.' She pointed to the door, holding a handkerchief to her streaming eyes with the other hand.

He went away quite convinced that as Falkner's prime suspect Mrs Pomfret was a non-starter—and considerably exercised in his mind about this manuscript. Scrope must be Scrope Davies, whose main claim to fame was that he was a friend of Lord Byron. A manuscript then—an old manuscript with mention of Scrope's name, and starting with the city of Aberdeen where, if he wasn't much mistaken, Byron had spent his early years. It didn't take much imagination to make a guess

141

at what this manuscript could be. It seemed too far fetched to be mentioned yet to Detective Chief Superintendent Falkner, but Charter felt some excitement at the possibility that the manuscript in Professor Pomfret's package could conceivably have been a copy of the Byron memoirs.

CHAPTER NINETEEN

There mark what ills the scholar's life assail.

JOHNSON

Charter went back to Falkner.

'If she's the killer I'm the King of Siam.'

'You're not. For one thing I shouldn't think she knows anything about the effect of immersion in cold water on the timing of the onset of rigor. What about the package? Did she open it?'

'She did and she says it was an old manuscript. She also said the money was in the briefcase on Friday, but when he brought it back from Southwell with the package the money was gone.'

'So the money was paid out in return for the manuscript.'

'What sort of manuscript would be worth that sort of money? And if that's what happened, where is the manuscript now?'

'Stolen by the murderer? Burned on the bonfire?'

'If it was stolen by the murderer then the murderer must also be the man who sold it to Pomfret. No one else would know he had it. He went straight to his room, to the lecture, and back to his room.'

'He might have talked about it beforehand. Or the seller might have talked.'

'He may have stayed away from the banquet not because he felt ill but to gloat over his purchase or perhaps to sell it on to a third party.'

'Why should he sell it? He'd paid a fortune for it. He wanted it for himself. A man of his wealth wouldn't be in a transaction like that just to make a small profit.'

'It looks as if he bought the manuscript in Southwell. You'd have thought Melbourne Hall a more likely place, but he had it with him before he set off for Melbourne Hall.'

'Have you any idea what the manuscript might be? Did she know?'

'She had no idea. But it must be something outstanding. We'll need some academic help on this one.'

'A bit tricky. We could be consulting the killer.'

'It's no good going to Nottingham University. Any expert in the Romantic field will be here for the conference. And even if he isn't he might still be involved.'

'Let's have Martin Proctor in. He might know.' Falkner picked up the phone. 'He's on his way. Now let's get this clear. This transaction we're imputing to the professor seems to me a bit off for a distinguished American professor who happens also to be a multi-millionaire. He's buying secretly, not on the open market and paying in a way that will enable him to keep the whole thing dark. There must be a very strong compulsion at work. What could possibly be that important to him?'

'He told me that he had a project on hand that would prove the value of his work. It seems some American university departments have more or less been taken over by a sort of McCarthyism of the Left. If you don't get on their bandwagon your students strike against you and you probably lose your job and no one will publish you. He was under strong compulsion to assert himself in some way and although he wouldn't do a shady deal for money he might for applause. He'd been used to it all his life. But it would have to be something as important as the Byron memoirs to make a real splash in the academic world.'

'The Byron memoirs! My God!'

Martin came into the room.

'Thank you for coming to join us, Mr Proctor,' said Falkner. 'Can you give us your opinion as an expert witness? We've got a mysterious and very valuable old manuscript and we need to know what it could be. Can you tell us anything about the Byron memoirs? Is there any possibility that they still exist and might be found?'

'You can't mean it,' said Martin. 'You might have a copy here? A copy of the memoirs?'

Falkner was soothing. 'The vaguest possibility,' he said. 'And we haven't got them here. If it was the memoirs they've disappeared again.'

'And may very well have been burned again,' put in Charter.

Falkner looked at him sharply. 'Our hoaxer. The bonfire. Maybe. Well, Mr Proctor?'

'Apparently several people made copies of the memoirs before they were burned. They were all told to destroy them but there's no evidence of whether they all did or whether they were lent around to friends who might have made surreptitious copies of them. The women of that period seem to have spent half their time copying out reams of poetry and prose for their lovers. It's certainly not impossible that one of those copies or a part of a copy might turn up in some muniment room. But you know, I'm not an expert witness on this one. You ought to consult the academics. What about Kenworthy?'

'We'll do that. At this stage we just need a quick run down on the possibilities.'

'Some muniment room,' said Charter

thoughtfully. 'What about Melbourne Hall? Pomfret dashed up there on Saturday.'

'I don't see why not. The Lambs lived there at the time. George Lamb was a friend of Byron and Mrs George Lamb was one of Lady Byron's supporters.'

'Would she have been interested in the memoirs?'

'She'd have been interested in anything that could have been used to discredit Byron.'

'And could this Mrs George Lamb have got hold of a copy of the memoirs?'

'I don't see why not. Mrs George Lamb lived in a cottage in the village of Melbourne after she was widowed so her papers might well be at Melbourne Hall. I suppose Lady Byron might have showed her or lent her the copy.'

'And she'd have made her own copy.'

'Let's get back to the professor,' said Falkner. 'Would he want the memoirs?'

'Of course he'd want them. It would be the find of the century. Do you remember all the excitement about the discovery of the letters and papers in the trunk belonging to Scrope Davies that they found a few years ago in a cellar at Barclays Bank? This would be far more important.'

'And worth a lot of money?'

'The copyright in the memoirs would probably belong to John Murray. The professor certainly wouldn't be after them for their monetary value.'

146

'Wouldn't John Murray forbid publication?'

'Oh, I doubt it. If the professor had done the work on them and presented Murrays with a *fait accompli*.'

'But would he be willing to pay a lot of money for them?'

'I imagine he'd pay anything it would take. The Pomfret fortune is comparable to the Duponts.'

Charter asked, 'But would he be entitled to them from a scholarly point of view? He was a Coleridge man. He'd want them in order to produce a scholarly edition with his own commentary, wouldn't he? But in the normal course of events he wouldn't be asked to do that would he?'

'No. Professor Marchand would be called in, or Professor McGann. He'd be poaching on their preserves.'

'Then why would the seller approach Pomfret?' asked Falkner. 'He was the wrong man.'

'No he wasn't,' said Charter. 'He may have been the wrong scholar but he was the man with the money. I don't suppose the seller thought for a minute that the right man would be tempted by an obviously shady transaction.'

'Pomfret would have done a pretty good job,' said Martin. 'He wasn't exclusively concerned with Coleridge. But I can't believe in any of this. Michael Pomfret was the most upright man you could hope to meet.'

'He was a distressed and worried man,' said Charter. 'Martin, do you think the manuscript could have come from Melbourne Hall? Pomfret rushed straight up there after he came back to the Saracen's Head with the package. The only reason I can think of for him to dash up there when he had a very tight schedule with a lecture to deliver a couple of hours later would be to check on the provenance.'

'He'd hardly be likely to buy them without a thorough history of the provenance. Anyway on your theory he'd already bought them. What was the use of dashing to Melbourne Hall? If he found he'd been sold a pup and they didn't come from there it was too late to get his money back.'

'I think I can understand that,' said Charter. 'He wanted the manuscript he was offered to be genuine so he swallowed whatever story he was given about the provenance without checking up on it. He was risking a sum of money that was extremely large by most standards but that he wouldn't really miss. But on learning where the manuscript came from he went up there to set his mind at rest. Perhaps to check on whether the bloke who sold it to him had really spent enough time up there to have found the manuscript. Or perhaps just to prowl around and look at the books and the archives with all the possibilities in view. I can quite see him doing that.'

'On the other hand,' said Falkner drily, 'he may have gone there simply to check some references for his talk.'

'If the Kerrs knew it was there,' said Charter, 'they would either have put the memoirs on the market or made it available to scholars.'

'Someone may have found them in the archives and abstracted them without a word to the Kerrs,' suggested Martin.

'Well, thank you, Mr Proctor,' said Falkner. 'You've been a great help. I needn't say that we'd like you to be discreet about this conversation.'

'Of course.'

'Just one more thing, Martin,' said Charter, 'can you think of any legitimate reason for Professor Pomfret to be carrying a briefcase full of Swiss francs?'

'Unless he was planning to do a moonlight flit to get away from Emmie, no I can't.' And he turned away. As he reached the door he turned back. 'Yes,' he said, 'I can think of a reason. It could be to do with the secret universities. He and Kenworthy were both involved in fund-raising for that project. It's just possible that he got a supply of francs to bank in Switzerland for the fund. It might be a good thing tax-wise to keep the fund there.'

'You don't think he would have half a million or so of his own money with him in Swiss francs?'

'No,' said Martin, 'not unless he wanted to buy something *sub rosa*. A thing I still can't believe of him.'

After he had gone Falkner looked at Charter.

'A Swiss bank account?'

'It's a possible explanation.'

'Possible explanation my foot,' said Falkner inelegantly. 'We haven't a shred of evidence on the memoirs and it may be something else. But I'm convinced that there's something in this scenario even if we haven't got it right yet. Enough anyway to go on all night with this if necessary. We're covering a lot of ground.'

'Then let's get on with the brainstorming.'

'Right. I'll get the beer this time.'

CHAPTER TWENTY

And Gold but sent to keep the fools in play,
For some to heap, and some to throw away.

POPE

When he came back Falkner said, 'Right. What sort of guy are we looking for and is there anyone here who fills the bill?'

'Someone greedy who was after a big price for the manuscript?'

'If the scrap of paper you rescued from the bonfire is big enough and not ruined by immersion the lab may be able to help us on the manuscript. If it is something seriously valuable then we're looking for someone who is probably seriously short of money.'

'Or to whom large amounts of money are either necessary because he is used to having large amounts of it or extremely desirable because he isn't.'

'Who have we got in the first category? Matthew Frost, Mrs Pomfret, Victoria Tallent. And in the second, Hellvellyn, Mr and Mrs Wallace, Martin Proctor, the Tierneys.'

'I reckon Martin is comfortably off and not greedy but we only met last Friday.'

'We'll start with Frost. Stinking rich. Nonstarter I'd have thought unless his empire is shaky. That must be checked. He has an alibi for Saturday night. But he could have had an accomplice.'

'The son-in-law, Andrew Tierney?'

'Possible. He has a record. No recurrence but it's still a black mark. I can't for the life of me see a motive for Frost. He's coming back this evening and I'll talk to him tomorrow. What about his daughter? Unless they alibi each other—the husband and wife.'

'I doubt if they do. He has a mistress.'

'Corinna Tierney wasn't taking part in the conference so she would be free to move about. Her statement has her in the kitchens and then in her room doing a quick change. But she got to the reception before the mayor. The staff corroborate all that.'

'I can corroborate it too. She couldn't have done it herself unless she had an accomplice.'

'The husband? Or perhaps a conspiracy with Matthew Frost in it with them?'

'Never.'

'We'll set it down as a possible plot between husband and wife.'

'Noting *en passant* that Matthew Frost has been spending time working at Melbourne Hall on a paper he wants to deliver to RPS.'

'Duly noted.'

'The snag about the possible plot between husband and wife is that they are not on good terms.'

'That needn't rule out a plot for their mutual benefit. A sudden access of cash might enable them to separate and live comfortably apart. If they detest each other it must be purgatory being tied together by the job of running a hotel.'

'Then they remain on the list of possibilities.'

'And slightly ahead of Matthew Frost.'

'Mrs Tallent made a fortune on the stock market. She couldn't conceivably have done the hoaxes herself or made the bonfire or moved the body. She is completely ruled out unless she hired help.'

'Ruled out anyway. If she wanted more money she'd surely have got it in the same way

152

she got the rest of it. By playing the markets.'

'Agreed. On to the less well off.'

'Lord Hellvellyn?'

'Motive: greed.'

'Psychologically and physically capable of violence?'

'I would have thought possibly so. As a matter of fact his two attendant ladies watch him all the time as if he were a little mad. Perhaps he is unbalanced.'

'Alibi?'

'The same as all the rest of RPS. We were all at the reception followed by the banquet.'

'Yes. I've got a team doing nothing but taking statements about the timing of those two events and who was where and who saw who doing what. But it's going to take time to get it all on the computer. Accomplice?'

'The wife and sister behave like his two handmaids. If he needed help they'd help him.'

'We'll keep him on the list. Martin Proctor?'

'It seems to me in the highest degree unlikely that a man like Martin would do murder for money, or kudos. And he has an alibi welcoming the mayor. But he could have had an accomplice, and of all the people involved in this affair there's no question he's physically the most likely hoaxer and murderer. But psychologically, no. I'd almost stake my career on it, but not quite.'

'What about the journalist?'

'Finn?'

153

'He's an odd sort of bloke. Can you rule him out? What's he doing at an affair like this?'

'Evidently he's made a corner in pieces on the Romantic Poets. Psychologically and physically capable? I'd have thought physically, yes, but psychologically, no. He's an easy-going Irishman. I can't see him going to such lengths as our hoaxer/murderer. He laughs too much.'

'According to Martin Proctor's statement he had left Venice by the time of the boat incident. He has the same alibi as well as the rest of you for the murder period. Motive?'

'He's a successful freelance. I can't see him going to all that trouble to get more money. But he may long for power and position and all the other things money can bring.'

'We'll keep him on the list. Lavinia Wallace?'

'She seems capable and cold. She behaves badly to Ninian. Puts him down in public and lets it be known that she earns more money than he does. Perhaps she resents the fact that she has to work.'

'On the list then. Ninian Wallace?'

'A distinct possibility. Disappointed at losing the chairmanship of the society to Martin Proctor. Doesn't earn enough for Lavinia. Physically capable of both the hoaxes and the moving of the body. But violence? I doubt it. On the other hand Martin seems to think he panics in an emergency and this murder does seem to have been the result of panic in an emergency.'

'Alibi?'

'Same as all the rest.'

'Accomplice?'

'Not the wife, I'd have thought. Martin Proctor? There's a thought for you! Or some hired thief who lost his head?'

'On the list then. Andrew Tierney?'

'There's the conviction for forgery.'

'That's very persuasive to me. This man we're looking for is dishonest in exactly the same way Andrew Tierney is dishonest. The motive? Greed.'

'And the chance of escaping from his humiliating position of accepting everything he owns from his wife or his father-in-law. That could be a very strong motive. Again, rivalry with his wife who could throw him out without a penny if she chose.'

'Not nowadays. He could sue her for a huge chunk of all she had.'

'So he could and undoubtedly would. But there's still a feeling of public disgrace about doing it. Or so many men would still feel. I reckon he'd much rather go for the jackpot on the quiet.'

'It's late, we'd better break this up. This is turning out to be useful and tomorrow we may have some more facts to go on.'

'I thought I'd see if Professor Kenworthy is still about and have a word with him about the memoirs. And then in the morning I could talk to Victoria Tallent.'

'Would you fancy taking a trip to Melbourne Hall and see what you can dig up about the memoirs?'

'Glad to.'

'Good, I'll leave the literary side of this investigation to you. We may soon have our answer from the lads who are looking for the tape. The Swiss francs have vanished into thin air. Or on to the hoaxer's bonfire.'

'He'll have used some sort of device for distorting his voice.'

'All the same it'll be the lab who'll get him in the end. You'll see.'

* * *

Charter found Kenworthy sitting alone in the bar drinking whisky and looking morose. The barman was patiently tidying up and washing glasses and trying hard not to look too often at the clock.

'Professor Kenworthy,' said Charter, 'would you play the expert witness for me? My colleagues have asked me to find out whether you can help us.'

Kenworthy stared at him unsmiling.

'Sit down,' he said. 'Whisky?'

Charter shook his head.

'How can I help?'

The light had gone out of the man. Until

today he had shown an easy friendliness. Now his eye was almost antagonistic. Had the death of the professor had such an effect on him? Or was it too much whisky?

'I need to know,' he explained, 'whether you think it's possible that a copy of Byron's memoirs could have turned up at Melbourne Hall and been purchased by Professor Pomfret in a rather underhand way.'

'I can't comment on what Professor Pomfret might feel compelled to do. The memoirs? It's always possible that a copy might be unearthed somewhere one day. Melbourne Hall is no more unlikely than anywhere else. There are plenty of connections with Byron there. But I would hardly think it likely either.'

'Could you suggest an explanation of how they might have got there?'

'It would be a waste of time. One could invent explanations of how they might have arrived at one of any number of possible places. Without the document itself you can't begin to talk about the provenance.'

'So you couldn't make a guess?'

'Not without seeing it. Have you got it to show me?'

'No. The chances are that it's gone up in smoke.'

'I see. Burned again.'

'That doesn't distress you?'

'No point in being distressed until we know that it was genuine.'

157

Charter gave up. 'I'll let you get off to bed,' he said. 'It's getting late.'

'Thanks for the hint. I'm going out for a walk first.' He got up and walked rather carefully out of the room and Charter heard the front door open and shut.

Could this be the reaction of a man who had panicked in the middle of a planned theft and hit out hard enough to kill? Was he dwelling on that level of horror? Or was he simply morose because he had lost a colleague and spent the evening drinking too much whisky to dull the edge of that grief?

Charter went to bed in some concern and wrote a brief report to leave for his colleague.

CHAPTER TWENTY-ONE

A light broke in upon my brain.

BYRON

Charter went out to the stableyard at six next morning and found Corinna's father leading out of a stall the chestnut Charter had ridden on the day of his arrival. Matthew Frost was a heavily built man in his early fifties with cropped black hair flecked with grey, very bright blue eyes, a red face and a heavy double chin. He wore riding breeches and hacking jacket over an open-necked shirt with a silk

158

cravat.

'Good morning,' he said. 'Riding?'

'I planned to help Corinna with the exercising.'

'Corinna's too busy and Andrew's too idle. Do you know Corinna's mare? Get her tacked up but be quick; I'll walk this one round but not for long.

'What are you doing here?' asked Frost as they walked their horses past the Lower Lake. 'Giving a paper?'

Charter eyed him narrowly. It was unlikely that he hadn't seen the papers with Finn's account of the bomb scare and the pictures of Charter.

'No, sir, I'm a policeman. I came to help Martin Proctor catch a hoaxer. Unfortunately I haven't yet succeeded and unfortunately for Martin this conference is becoming something of a nightmare.'

'It's his job to run this conference.'

'His unpaid job, sir.'

Frost looked at him sharply and Charter thought he saw a glint of admiration. Like many rich and powerful men Matthew Frost was used to being grovelled to and could respect anyone who refused to grovel.

'The police made any progress?'

'Yes. We're doing fairly well. My being on the scene has saved time.'

'I see.'

'Have you any idea, sir, who might have

killed the professor?'

'I have no idea whatsoever. That's your job not mine.'

'Shall we trot them on?'

They trotted on. A couple of geese were honking gently. A moorhen scuttered away from the edge of the lake. A pale yet radiant sun hung above the gardens behind them.

Charter decided to goad his companion. 'My colleagues will want to talk to you today about your movements on Saturday.'

Frost cast him a cold glance. 'I was entertaining clients,' he said. 'They stopped with me at my house and I was with them until they left yesterday.'

Without warning he put his horse into a canter. Charter's mare shied. He managed to hold her and followed in a controlled rather than a headlong canter. Not the best circumstances for questioning a witness. On the other hand this was illuminating as regards character. Frost swung into a woodland ride, cleared a log across the track then put his mount at a formidable gate. On landing he went straight into a gallop without a backward glance to check that all was well with Charter who followed him over the jump. After a while Frost pulled up and turned for home.

'As they're stabled don't they need an hour?' asked Charter.

'They're not getting an hour today. I've people to meet, talks to have, the international committee meeting.'

'And my colleagues will want to see you as soon as possible.'

'That's why half an hour will do today. You can tell them I'll see them after I've breakfasted, I'll keep my counsel till then. I've no intention of being interrogated more than once. Or by an odd policeman who turns up here.'

They walked the horses back in silence and Frost put his mount in the stables and went into the hotel. Charter rubbed both horses down and gave them water and hay nets. He went to shower and change, then looked for Victoria Tallent and joined her at breakfast.

'Good morning, dear,' she said. 'These are bad times we're living through. Murder in the society. That poor dear man. I could hear every word of his lectures. He knew how to project his voice. None of the young ones can. Do you know, he came to my ceremony for the plaque to Shelley in Poland Street and he said it would remind people of Shelley and make them read his poetry. He was just a bit naive, dear man. Who killed him?'

'I want to ask you about a manuscript he bought on Saturday for a great deal of money. There's talk of it being part of a copy of Byron's memoirs.'

'How marvellous. Where did he get it?'

'Possibly in the archives at Melbourne Hall. Do you think that's possible?'

'Well, the Lamb family lived there. I don't think it could be Lord Melbourne or Caroline Lamb or George Lamb but Lady Byron was great friends with George Lamb's wife Caroline. She was called Caro George to distinguish her from William Lamb's wife who was also called Caroline—Caro William. Perhaps a copy of the memoirs might have got to Melbourne Hall through Caro George. Lady Byron had a copy of the memoirs which Byron sent to her but she sent it back unopened. I've always thought she must have peeked. She was obsessed with justifying herself over the separation and I've always believed she must have copied out the bits she thought might be helpful to her case and hidden them away for later use. I don't believe she could have resisted the temptation to open the package and read what Byron wrote about her in the memoirs. She wasn't an honourable woman. Well, you have to make allowances for her. Women weren't expected to be honourable in those days. The dear little creatures were supposed to be frail and fragile and up to all sorts of tricks to keep their end up.'

'So, might Lady Byron have taken a copy of the memoirs to Melbourne Hall?'

'Oh no. She was never invited there. Lady Byron might have let Caro George see her copy but she would never have let her take it away. For one thing she had told Byron she hadn't read it and she would never have admitted to a lie.'

'So you think Melbourne Hall is out?'

'No. I think Caro George might have made a copy but she wouldn't have got the copy of the memoirs from Lady Byron. She could have got it from Henry Brougham.'

'Brougham, the lawyer?'

'Yes. Brougham was one of Lady Byron's legal advisers so she might have shown the memoirs to him and he could have shown the copy to Caro George and she could have made a copy. It's odd that she detested Byron so much because he wrote a rather charming poem about her singing.'

'But why should Brougham show it to George Lamb's wife?'

'Because they had an affair of the heart in Geneva. It was probably over by 1817 but they might still have been seeing each other. Lady Byron would have been furious with Brougham if she knew, but Brougham was quite unscrupulous and he hated Byron and did all he could to shoot him down at the time of the scandal. Brougham would have enjoyed chortling over the memoirs with Caro George. He ended up a good lawyer but he wasn't a good man.'

'It seems a possible scenario though it's a bit unfair to impute all this underhand behaviour to Brougham and Caro George without a shred of evidence.'

'I shouldn't worry about that. It's only a bit of their own medicine. They both spread horrendous rumours about Byron for sheer malice.'

'So there could have been a copy of parts of the memoirs lying about in the archives at Melbourne Hall for all these years?'

'There could have been. What have you done with it?'

'I'm afraid it's disappeared.'

She looked at him hard.

'Professor Pomfret was killed for it?'

'Let's say simply that I don't think the copy of the memoirs is going to appear again. If it ever did.'

'It's disappointing but you can't really worry too much about that with the poor man lying dead.'

'No. You can't. Will you please keep quiet about this conversation? Until I tell you it's safe?'

'Yes. It would cause a lot of chatter.'

Charter headed for Melbourne Hall, driving through a magical early morning landscape, rolling fields receding in rank on rank of sunlit grass and leafy shaws. He parked between the church and the Hall, walked through the stableyard and craft centre to the estate office and was shown into a large room where the archivist was busy at a large scrubbed table laden with neat piles of documents.

They sat at the table and a handsome young

woman brought coffee and biscuits.

'Now,' said the archivist, 'I'm to understand that you suspect someone may have found a copy of the Byron memoirs lurking somewhere here and quietly abstracted them and sold them.'

'If it can be established it will explain a lot and might help us to find the killer of Professor Pomfret.'

'Very odd that business of the hoaxes and next day the murder. I was very sorry to hear it. He was here only on Saturday. A very pleasant man.'

'Did you talk to him and can you tell me why he came?'

'It was an unexpected visit. We were rather surprised because the whole society was coming that afternoon for tea. But I suppose he felt he couldn't make enquiries about books and research during a social occasion.'

'So what did he do when he arrived?'

'He simply came into the estate office and asked if he could look at some books in the library.'

'Do you know which books?'

'No. I took him over to the library and waited with him. He walked about and picked out a book or two in a rather desultory way it seemed to me.'

'Did he talk to you while he was doing this?'

'Yes he did. He was interested to know which members of the Coleridge and Other

Romantic Poets Society had been here over the last year.'

'And how many had?'

'Professor Kenworthy used to come regularly. Apart from him there was only Matthew Frost. He was doing some research in the library.'

'How long ago?'

'He started coming about eighteen months ago and he still comes occasionally. He was preparing a paper to read to the society but it obviously isn't finished yet. He would have asked my wife and me to hear it and there's been no mention of that.'

'Do you know the subject of the paper?'

'It was to do with George Lamb. He made a study of the books we have here belonging to Mrs George Lamb, and a rather amusing thing happened. He found some papers between the leaves of one of her books—*Letters of a Hindu Rajah* by Eliza Hamilton (1801). They were pages from a sort of diary, but not in Caro George's handwriting. Mr Frost thought they were pages from the memoirs of Byron and got quite excited. He insisted on our searching for more of them and then he rushed up to London with them. Lord Ralph was abroad at the time so he went to someone in London and found that they were nothing of the kind.'

'Did he indeed?' said Charter frowning. 'I don't like the sound of that at all.'

The archivist looked distressed. 'I'm quite

sure Mr Frost would never try to defraud Lord Ralph.'

'Don't mention it to anyone,' said Charter.

'I'll mention it to no one else but I'll have to tell Lord Ralph. He'll be extremely put out.'

'I must have a word with him about it when he gets back.'

'Lord Ralph will be sorry not to have seen you. He's in London today. He was distressed to hear of the professor's death. They had met in the States.'

On his return Charter found Falkner at the Ravenshead forward post checking with the incident room.

'Be with you in ten minutes,' said Falkner. 'We've got another professor missing. We're trying to get hold of the one who left on Sunday to make sure he arrived safely. I'm hoping we haven't got a serial killer of English Literature professors on our hands.'

'It's not Kenworthy?'

'Yes I'm afraid it is. His things are still in his room but he didn't sleep in his bed last night and he's not to be found this morning.'

'He went out for a walk last night after I left. He was in a strange mood. And he didn't mention that he spent some time at Melbourne Hall doing research.'

'He could be our man?'

'I'd have staked a lot on his being nothing of the kind. But now I don't know. I hope he hasn't pitched himself into the lake.'

'I've got the frogmen out in case someone else pitched him in.'

Falkner went back into the incident room and reappeared five minutes later.

'We've tracked down Professor Kristeller and I've just had a word with him. He's back in Vermont. He claims that he left because, when he was insulted by a journalist, the chairman of the society and his deputy did nothing to defend him. Also they had turned down the paper he offered for the conference and he was thoroughly disgruntled. He practically had a heart attack on the phone when I told him about the death of Professor Pomfret and offered to come straight back. I told him it wouldn't be necessary at this stage but to stop where he is. I think he's not our man. He checked out quite openly. He claimed that he had to stay for Pomfret's talk as they are colleagues but once that was over he felt he could go. He sat through the bomb scare but it was the last straw. He claims to suffer from claustrophobia and the experience was very unpleasant for him even though they weren't in fact shut in for long.

'Right,' he said, 'back to the North of Trent. I want to be on the spot when we find Kenworthy. *If* we find Kenworthy.'

'Have you interviewed Matthew Frost yet?'

'No. He was very rude to my PC this morning so I've left him to kick his heels. We'll have him in as soon as we've had our little chat.'

'He's a difficult customer. I rode with him this morning. He's quite without compunction on a ride. Did his level best to get me on the floor. I can't help thinking that his way of riding out with a partner is rather reminiscent of the behaviour of our hoaxer.'

When they were installed in Corinna's office Falkner asked, 'So does your trip to Derbyshire change anything?'

'It points to Frost again,' said Charter. 'He's the only member of RPS who has been working at Melbourne Hall except for Kenworthy. Frost found some pages of an old diary in a book belonging to one of the great Regency ladies of the Lamb family who once lived there and jumped to the conclusion that what he'd found was a part of Byron's memoirs. He had it looked at in London and was told it was a sell. Nothing to do with Byron, so he told the archivist.'

'But only a few pages. And Pomfret got the lot.'

'So it was a fake cooked up with the help of those two pages.'

'Looks like it. And that was the first thing that occurred to Kenworthy when I talked to him. He simply assumed that the first thing was whether the manuscript was genuine.'

'That's it. And of course it wasn't. That's why the man who sold it to the professor went to steal it back that night. He'd faked the memoirs well enough to stand up to scrutiny for one evening in a bad light but he knew the professor would soon find out he'd been had. The theft was supposed to look like another hoax.'

'So that's the reason for the whole series of hoaxes.'

'To make the professor see the theft of the manuscript as just another hoax.'

'Does it fit? Yes, I'm sure it does. The first hoax is the spectacular one in Venice. It has to be spectacular to impress it on the society so that they will recognize the later hoaxes as part of a series. The second one is on Martin because he is the chairman.'

'The third is on the professor because he has to be made aware of the hoaxes by suffering one himself.'

'And it puts him in the frame of mind to expect further hoaxes and later on to see the theft of the memoirs as another.'

'So in fact the hoaxes weren't done to damage the society but to fox the professor. And the reason they were spread over such a long period was to allow our man to organize the faking of the memoirs. He had to get a reasonable text and then arrange the forgery.'

'But why kill the professor?'

'Perhaps the prof didn't know who he was buying from, so when the bloke was surprised by him he hit out in a panic because he didn't want to be recognized. We don't know that he intended murder.'

'He didn't call for help when he saw the man bleeding and unconscious.'

'Oh, we know he was no Little Lord Fauntleroy, but he hadn't planned murder. When things went wrong he made some lethal decisions. That's all we can say.'

'So what we've got isn't theft of the true memoirs but fraud with a faked copy to squeeze a large sum out of the professor. Someone who found papers he thought were part of the memoirs might very well think about the possibility of making that exciting prospect come true.'

'Except that he doesn't need the money. Let's have him in. And you take him, John.'

Matthew Frost came storming into the room in a rage.

'I sent you a message,' he said, 'that I could see you straight after breakfast. It's now twelve-thirty. I don't know what you're playing at but I'm a busy man. I have to get back to London.'

'We shan't keep you long, sir,' said Falkner mildly.

He nodded to Charter who asked, 'How much do you know, sir, about the hoaxes?'

'What everybody else knows of course. Someone put a bomb in that boat in Italy and then there was a bomb scare last night.'

'There has been another hoax on Professor Pomfret. Do you know anything about that?'

171

'I was here from late on Friday night until Saturday afternoon. I then went back to London and I came back late last night. Is it likely I'd know anything about what happened to Professor Pomfret during this conference?'

'The hoaxer could have used an accomplice. So being away from the conference doesn't at all constitute an alibi either for the hoaxes or the murder.'

'What was the hoax on the professor?'

'Someone persuaded him to buy a manuscript which he believed was a copy of Byron's memoirs.'

Frost's eyes narrowed. 'I don't believe it,' he said sharply.

'We are asking everyone present at the conference whether he or she had anything to do with faking a copy of the memoirs. What about you Mr Frost?'

'Why would I do such a thing?'

'For gain?'

'Do you know how much I'm worth?'

'No, Mr Frost, but I shall make it my business to find out.

'Did you spend some time researching at Melbourne Hall early this year?'

'Yes. I was preparing a lecture for RPS.'

'But you have not yet delivered the lecture?'

'No. It isn't finished.'

'When did you last go to Melbourne Hall?'

'About three months ago.'

'And how much of your study still remains

to be completed?'

'Most of it.'

'I see.'

'If you imagine a man like me would go in for fraud to trick an old friend like Professor Pomfret you're mad.'

'I believe Mrs Lavinia Wallace is your secretary?'

'Yes.'

'Is she also secretary of RPS?'

'Yes.'

'If you had planned to hoax the society would Mrs Wallace have been prepared to help you?'

'I refuse to answer a question based on such a premise.'

'It is true, isn't it, that Mrs Wallace could have written the letter inviting Bracousse to address the society and she could also have gone to the London Library on the day Professor Pomfret's papers were soaked in red ink?'

'She could have done both things but only a half-wit could possibly suspect that she did.'

'Someone typed that letter on paper with the RPS letterhead. And someone with access to the London Library, emptied a bottle of red ink over Professor Pomfret's paper. Mrs Wallace is the most likely person to have done these things. She has no motive for either and we consider that if she was involved it was under the direction of someone else. You are

173

her employer. I wonder whether you have anything to say about that?'

'Nothing at all. It's an outrageous suggestion.'

'Alternatively, if you were the hoaxer (and this is simply a speculation we must entertain about every member of your society) you might have had a different accomplice. What about Andrew Tierney?'

'Andrew? Do you imagine for a moment that I would enter into any sort of undertaking with that shower?'

'Your son-in-law, sir.'

'For God's sake what has that got to do with it? All the girls seem to suffer from *nostalgie de la boue* these days. What do you think he did?'

'That depends on whether he has an alibi.'

'Well you can ask Corinna about that can't you?'

'They do sleep together then?'

'Ask them. I don't have to stay and listen to this.' And he got up and stormed out of the room.

Falkner raised his eyebrows at Charter. 'You don't pull your punches do you?' he said and grinned. 'No way could I risk that sort of backchat with a local dignitary.'

'Well it hasn't achieved much. Just stirred up the waters.'

'He may have stormed out because we were getting too close. He may have seen that his going back to London that night to make sure

174

he had an alibi won't help him at all because we know he'd use an accomplice. Having sold the fake memoirs to Pomfret he'd never risk showing his face in the professor's bedroom and being caught stealing them back again. So what would he do? Fix up a fool-proof alibi for himself. After all it would be natural for a father to stop here that evening to be at his daughter's great evening doing the banquet for RPS.'

'And another thing that points to him: as her father, and probably a shareholder in the hotel, would it be likely that he'd spoil the daughter's part in it by putting something toxic in the food? It would be logical for him to choose the more difficult hoax of the bomb scare.'

'So when he's sitting it out in London and he hears of the murder, which he reckons must have been committed by his accomplice, what would he do? It must have been a shock.'

'He'd stay put for a while. A complete change of plan. If the murder hadn't happened I reckon he'd be in Zurich now, banking his ill-gotten gains.'

'He'd reckon it wouldn't be easy to bring it home to him unless the accomplice spoke up. He couldn't depend on the son-in-law. Could the daughter be the accomplice? Could she have panicked and hit the professor hard enough to kill him?'

'Very unlikely.'

'She's athletic and strong. She knows where

the gardener's stuff is kept. She knows the timing of the reception and the dinner precisely. She needs the money. She's a possibility. But to go back to Frost as the instigator, I don't see how the professor could be persuaded to pay a sum for the memoirs large enough to make a difference to the wealth of so wealthy a man as Frost. And to pay up without close scrutiny and authentification.'

'He'd pay up because he knew that the memoirs without strings were worth a lot more to him than the memoirs in the hands of John Murray.'

'I can see no motive for Frost unless he has a madman's grudge against the society, or the professor, or has lost all his money in a big bang.'

'I've heard no rumours about the Frost empire.'

'There are always rumours, especially up here. He's a local character since he bought the estate at Gonalston.'

'There's something at the back of my mind about that. Someone made a remark about his business acumen or lack of it. I can't for the life of me remember who it was but it will come to me. I have to say, Robert, that it's beginning to look very like Frost to me. You may have noticed that he made no mention of the discovery of the two pages of the memoirs at Melbourne Hall. Surely he'd have thought of them at once when the memoirs were mentioned.'

'I'm not sure about that. He was in a rage. He may have been too angry to think straight.'

'In that case we can expect him to come back to us on that one. In any case there's nothing we can do yet. We haven't a scrap of evidence.'

The telephone rang. Falkner picked up the telephone and listened.

'What flight number?' He wrote down the number and replaced the receiver.

'The Frenchman's been interviewed and he's leaving for Heathrow. As one of the victims of the hoaxes it's not likely that he comes into it and he has a lecture to give tonight in Paris.'

'So nothing useful?'

'Only one thing. He saw Matthew Frost and Lord Hellvellyn having the father and mother of a row. He was walking in the Japanese gardens and saw them sitting in one of those little wooden huts. It got heated and Hellvellyn was positively waving his arms about and Frost was obviously fobbing him off. He couldn't follow what they were saying but Hellvellyn was accusing Frost of something. We'll have to get them both in.'

'Would you object to my dashing off after Bracousse? It might help if I had a word with him.'

'Help yourself. Here's the flight number.'

CHAPTER TWENTY-TWO

What poet would not grieve to see,
His brethren write as well as he?

SWIFT

Charter caught up with Bracousse heading for Departures.

'Sir.' He walked along beside him. 'May I ask you a few questions? It may help us to find out who killed Professor Pomfret.'

'Of course. But quickly, please. I must go through.'

'I'll go through with you.' Charter held up his police identification. 'I'm told you overheard an argument between Lord Hellvellyn and Matthew Frost. Can you remember anything at all that was said? Any expression, a word, a name, might help.'

'Why can't you ask the two gentlemen?'

'We shall. But their accounts of the matter may not agree. We always need evidence from witnesses who are not concerned.'

'I see. I will think.' He frowned as he did so. Then his brow cleared. 'Yes,' he said. 'They talked about money—shares. It was a financial transaction. Lord Hellvellyn was not very pleased with Mr Frost.'

They had reached the gate. The stewardess said, 'Are you coming through sir? We'll be closing the flight any minute now.'

Bracousse turned to Charter. 'Yes,' he said, 'I know now what it was. They talked of Asian businessmen. And banks. The context seems clear: they were talking about the bank that went bankrupt—BCCI.'

'Thank you, sir. Have a good journey.'

The stewardess bore Bracousse away.

Charter drove back to the Abbey. Had Frost cheated Hellvellyn in some way over the collapse of BCCI? Was he connected in some way with the bank and its fall? Had he perhaps advised Hellvellyn to put his money into BCCI and was Hellvellyn blaming him for his losses?

And then he realized what was of much more significance to the investigation. Would Frost have advised Hellvellyn to put his money in that bank if he were not himself involved in it? And if he was involved was it not likely that he had lost money himself when the bank crashed? The only reason Frost was not at this moment prime suspect was his wealth, but if he had lost heavily in the BCCI crash then he might have a financial motive for faking and selling the manuscript of the memoirs.

The crash occurred before the incident in Venice last May. The timing would fit.

Either he had the idea of faking the memoirs to retrieve his losses and went to Melbourne Hall to work out the provenance, or he went to Melbourne Hall to work on his paper for RPS and there found the papers which gave him the idea for the fraud. The former seemed the more likely. If he was coping with a serious loss of fortune he would hardly have time or inclination for dilettante literary pursuits.

As he turned into the drive at Norman Abbey he smiled suddenly. He had remembered who it was who had talked about mistakes Frost had made in business. It was Mrs Victoria Tallent and before he went to see Falkner he would track her down and find out what she meant.

He had to postpone this plan for he found the Press back in full force, the conference members huddled together in shocked groups, the place swarming with uniformed and scene-of-crime men. The frogmen had found the body of Professor Kenworthy not in the lake but in the stewpond earlier in the afternoon and Falkner was too busy to be approached.

Martin came out to meet him and told him the last of the papers had been abandoned and everyone was waiting only for the word to set off for home.

Charter found Victoria sitting in the hotel garden with Dermot Finn drinking coffee.

'Come and join us,' said Victoria. 'What's the matter? You've had a shock.'

'This inquiry is dealing out shock after shock,' he said, non-committally. 'Finn, do you mind? I have to talk to Victoria.'

'Sit down, dear,' said Victoria. 'I'm just having a little rest. I get tired these days.'

Charter sat beside her.

'The police have been asking us all sorts of questions,' she said. 'They're everywhere. Looking through our things. Diving into the lake in those extraordinary costumes. Walking about with those beautiful dogs. I told them everything I could think of. What do you want to know?'

'You said Frost was a very clever businessman but that he sometimes makes mistakes. Had you any particular mistakes in mind?'

'Yes dear, of course. I was talking about his putting his money in BCCI. He mentioned it to me because we compare notes when we have a little flutter. He told me I'd get a much higher interest rate if I put my money in BCCI.'

'And did you?'

'Of course not. I'm much too hard-headed for that. I asked myself what the high interest rate was for and I didn't like the answers I gave myself. So I kept my money where it was. It doubles every seven years you know. I don't invest in anything risky. I know Matthew lost money in BCCI when it crashed. I'm afraid Lord Hellvellyn lost some too.'

'Did he indeed? And do you think Lord Hellvellyn was angry with Mr Frost because he advised him to invest in BCCI?'

'He ought not to be. He should have taken it with a pinch of salt as I did. Why should an English peer invest in an Asian bank? It was sheer greed.'

'Wasn't it sheer greed on Matthew Frost's part?'

'Well, I don't know about that. I don't call it greed for a business man to move his capital around to make money. He's a business man and he's got to do business. But Lord Hellvellyn isn't a business man, he's a poet.'

'Even poets have to try to make a living.'

'I know Wordsworth had to take that excise job but I don't think he would have put his money into a shady bank to get more interest and Lord Hellvellyn is much better off than Wordsworth was.'

'Then perhaps he'll have to live like Wordsworth for real and stop playing at it.'

Victoria looked at him with approval.

'I must say,' she told him, 'you are quite quick on the uptake.'

'Has Mr Frost ever mentioned to you a scheme for retrieving his finances?'

'Oh, I don't think it's as bad as that for him. He has so many irons in the fire. He's a Name at Lloyds, you know.'

'Do you feel up to answering any more questions?'

'To tell you the truth, dear, you look much tireder yourself than I feel now I've had a rest.'

'Did you hear anything during the night on Saturday after we all went back to bed?'

'No, not that night. But last night. I got up at about two and I heard a noise in the passage and I looked out and it was Ninian Wallace. He can't have been on his way to the loo because all the rooms have what they call facilities and I really would be disappointed in him if he was going visiting when he's got a perfectly beautiful wife of his own. So I watched to see what he did. He went downstairs and looked all round the hall and the kitchen. But it wasn't to make himself a cup of tea because there's all that in the rooms and anyway he came straight out again. And then he went to the front door and tried it. But it's always locked at night. You can ask for a key if you want one. So he stood for a while peering out into the courtyard and then he came upstairs again and I suppose he went back to bed.'

'Perhaps his wife was visiting.'

'He wasn't likely to find her in the kitchen if that's what he thought. Though he might have hoped she was foraging.'

'I must go and talk to my colleagues now. I'll come and see you again very soon.'

'That's all right. Off you go.'

He had caught a glimpse of Miss Cunningham walking through the garden to the edge of the lake and he decided now was the time to buttonhole one of Hellvellyn's guardian angels and get some solid information on their charge.

He fell into step beside her.

'How is he?' he asked, and she looked up at

him apprehensively.

'I can see there's something wrong with him,' he said. 'You and Lady Hellvellyn never leave him alone for a moment.'

'He's in one of his dark periods,' she began, then she looked at him and shook her head. 'No,' she said, 'I can't pretend any more. How did you guess?'

'It wasn't difficult. You and your sister were so obviously behaving like a team. The idea of a team of nurses sprang to mind almost at once. And you seemed so worried about him. What is it? Alzheimer's?'

'We aren't sure. There's been no diagnosis. We want to go on as we are as long as we can. But we have to watch him very carefully. He isn't violent but he does sometimes talk rather loudly. People who don't know how kind he is might get alarmed.'

'It's very good of you to bring him here. It must be a great strain on you and Lady Hellvellyn.'

'Oh it is, it is! It's so good of you to understand. And we've watched him. We were so glad we'd made a pact not to leave him for a moment. There's no question. We were with him all the time, I do assure you. And this later one, poor Professor Kenworthy. We haven't left him for a moment.'

'How long has he been like this?'

'It's been coming on for quite a long time. He gets morose and then he refuses to do the readings. We'll have to give them up altogether before long if he doesn't improve. Without them we would be quite broke. We only have our pensions. Lord Hellvellyn made some very unwise investments last year and we lost almost everything.'

'I'm sorry to hear it. Was it BCCI?'

'Yes, I'm afraid it was.'

'And it was Mr Frost who recommended BCCI to him?'

'Yes. The interest rates were so much higher, you see. I believe Mr Frost took most of his money out in time. Someone gave him what they call a tip off. But he had forgotten Lord Hellvellyn, or at least that's the most charitable way to interpret it. Stephen was in such a rage when he found out what had happened. We calmed him down but this conference has been a bit of a risk. We were worried about bringing him but he enjoys it so much. We didn't want to disappoint him.'

'And he did have the chance to tell Mr Frost what he thought of him, didn't he?'

'Oh you heard about that did you? There wasn't any danger, we were both within call. We met Mr Frost in the Japanese gardens. Stephen told us to leave them alone so we withdrew behind some shrubs. We knew it would be all right, Mr Frost is a strong, young man. Of course if it had been a woman or a young girl we wouldn't have moved a step.'

'And did Mr Frost apologize?'

185

'No, of course not. Business men like that have no conscience. They had a real slanging match and although it did no good from a practical point of view it cheered Stephen up no end. He had quite a good night after that.'

'Did Lord Hellvellyn know Professor Pomfret?'

'Only as an acquaintance. He doesn't mix much with the academics. They tend to be rather grudging about his poetry.'

'And you are quite sure he didn't have a queer turn and go to the professor's room?'

'Certainly not, Dorothy always locks the door of their bedroom and hides the key.'

'And he couldn't have got out and crept up on Professor Kenworthy?'

'And done him in? No, never, Mr Charter. It would be quite impossible. We are always there, you see. And we always will be.'

'Will you be able to manage?'

'Oh yes. We're preparing for the day he can't write any more and is too ill to give the readings. We're investing in bees and beehives. We're going to start a business in Lakeland honey. And we shall make things, you know, to sell. We're very good at tapestries and knitting and crochet, and with artistic labels and the cachet of the Hellvellyn name, we ought to make do. We never have to buy new clothes. We don't need them. We've always bought the very best quality so nothing wears out. We've always had our shoes. They go in to be serviced by the makers like cars. And we've got the goats' milk. It's particularly good for Lord Hellvellyn. And we have rows and rows of potatoes and beans. He loves digging. I don't know why I'm telling you all this. And you know, there's every chance that we'll get some compensation one of these days.'

'I tell you what, Miss Cunningham, I'll commission you to do some water-colours for me. That's the way to make money.'

'Do you think they would sell on their own?'

'I'm quite sure they would. I'll come up and see them one day and bring an American friend who goes in for that sort of thing and we'll talk about it.

'Miss Cunningham, may I ask you one question for myself? You may think it intolerably impertinent.'

'How very alarming. But please do ask anything you like.'

'Where and when did the title appear in the family? Was it a poetic peerage? Is there a Poet Laureate ancestor? Or was it something quite different?'

She laughed aloud. 'Oh no,' she said, 'nothing like that. It was simply an ancestor who met George the Third on that first visit to Cheltenham that put Cheltenham on the map. Lord Hellvellyn's ancestor was visiting a friend down there and when he was presented to the Royal party he happened to be able to give the King some good farming tips. He farmed the

187

Grange. The land has all been sold off long ago. But he was a good scientific farmer for those days and he and Farmer George used to get into a huddle together and talk farming. That was absolutely the most he ever did to earn his peerage. We think it must have been in one of his disturbed periods that the King had him ennobled.'

'That's interesting. Finn would make a lot of that. Did he manage to interview Lord Hellvellyn before all this started?'

She swung round fiercely.

'Dermot Finn? I wouldn't let Dermot Finn near him. We made him promise he wouldn't bother Lord Hellvellyn as long as Dorothy and I talked to him up there at Grasmere. And so we did and he sent a photographer. But he promised faithfully not to try to interview Stephen if we came to the conference.'

'These journalists! He distinctly told me he was here to interview Lord Hellvellyn and that Lord Hellvellyn had agreed to be interviewed.'

'He was lying. Stephen is never interviewed. It upsets him. And anyway we would never allow it. One never knows what he might say.'

Charter went away much chastened at the intolerance of his earlier attitude to these admirably staunch old ladies and their charge.

He went back to Falkner blazing with excitement. 'Anything on Frost?' Falkner asked.

'Circumstantial still, but persuasive,' said

Charter. 'It looks as if both Hellvellyn and Frost may have put money into BCCI. Frost advised both Hellvellyn and Victoria Tallent to do it. So it's quite on the cards that he lost a great deal of money over a year ago which would fit in very nicely with the timing of the hoaxes and give plenty of time for the preparation of the fraud.'

'A scenario that applies equally well to Lord Hellvellyn.'

'He's out. Incapable. The reason his ladies chaperone him as they do is that he's well on the way to senile dementia.'

'Poor chap.'

'So let's stick to Frost for the moment. Another thing that may be relevant. Mrs Tallent tells me she saw Ninian Wallace searching for his wife last night between two and three a.m. That is, she assumed it was his wife he was looking for: I'll go and talk to him. It may be significant that Matthew Frost, who had to go back to London on Saturday you may remember, came back early on Monday. Perhaps Mrs Wallace may have joined him in his room.'

'Mrs Frost didn't come with him?'

'Apparently she doesn't care for academic or business conferences and leads a full life at Gonalston with her dogs and horses.'

'Would you care to find out whether Andrew Tierney's alibi for Saturday night holds? Not a job for a tactless young PC. And also we need to know if any of his clothes are missing.'

Charter drove back to the hotel and found Corinna in the stables.

'Come and sit down for a few minutes,' he said, and she put her hayfork down and came with him into the stableyard where they sat down on bales of straw.

'Look,' he said, 'I didn't intend to deceive you. I was asked to come here to track this hoaxer down. My job was to protect you all from the joker. I wouldn't have stood a chance if I had told you all who I am and what I was doing.'

'Why did you choose to be a policeman?' asked Corinna. 'I'd have thought it would be the last thing.'

'I wanted to be a novelist but I can't write. So I decided on the police.'

'Why?'

'A policeman needs the same qualities as a novelist apart from a good prose style.'

'And are you glad you chose it?'

'It hasn't worked out too badly. A Detective Chief Superintendent is more important than you'll ever know.'

'Next thing I suppose you'll have to interrogate me.'

'No. If you prefer it Chief Superintendent Falkner can do it.'

'It's all right. What do you want to know?'

'Are any of Andrew's clothes missing?'

She stared at him blankly then said, 'Ask

Daisy Masters.'

'This is serious. I do need an answer.'

'Well, if you can wait a few minutes I'll go and see if anything seems to be missing. But I might not know. I could ask him.'

'That wouldn't answer the purpose.'

She looked at him sharply then got up and went into the hotel. In less than five minutes she was back again.

'No,' she said. 'As far as I can tell there isn't a single thing missing.'

'Thank you.' He didn't believe for a moment that she had looked. 'And you can give him an alibi for Saturday night?'

'What?' She gave him a hard look then said, 'Of course I can. Yes.' And, picking up the hayfork, she went back into the stables.

He walked out on to the grass facing the Abbey. Its stonework was both pale and bright in the sunshine. The lake was still as glass. A flock of white geese were walking solemnly along the banks towards the Garden Lake.

Sophie came and stood beside him.

'How is it going?' she asked. 'I'd never have asked you to do it if I'd know it would turn out like this. I didn't want to spoil your holiday.'

'Don't worry. We'll have him before long.'

'I believe you're enjoying it.'

'I want to finish it and stop this man. Kenworthy's dead, you know. That's why the grounds are cordoned off up there by the stewpond. Someone hit him over the head and

191

pushed him in. Don't wander off on your own with your cameras, Sophie.'

'How rotten. I can't believe it. I don't know how you can stand it, John.'

'No,' he told her, 'neither do I.' He left her then and drove over to Ravenshead where he found Falkner talking to the head of the Technical Support Unit.

'I'll be with you in half an hour,' Falkner said.

CHAPTER TWENTY-THREE

And, if she move unquietly,
Perchance, 'tis but the blood so free
Comes back and tingles in her feet.
No doubt, she hath a vision sweet.

COLERIDGE

'So,' Falkner said when they were installed in the office again. 'Not a petty forger like Tierney; a brilliant scholar in Kenworthy to fake the script and they would have found an experienced forger to make it look good. Kenworthy must have got a large cut of the proceeds. But once he began to suspect murder had been done they couldn't be sure he wouldn't talk so they killed him.'

'It would need very strong nerves to go after him with us here in force. As risky as moving

Pomfret to the Slype. It's the same man all right. Did I tell you Kenworthy went out for a walk after our talk? Someone followed him out in the dark.'

'Blow on the back of the head with a blunt instrument which hasn't been found yet. Thrown into the stewpond to drown. But full report after the PM.'

'He did fake the memoirs I suppose.'

'It looks like it.'

'He was morose with me yesterday. He must have been working out what had happened and what he ought to do. He may have talked to the hoaxer who realized he might pull the plug on them.'

'Then the next thing is to find out who he talked to. Who were his cronies?'

'Let's have Martin in.'

Martin had nothing to say on this subject.

'I'm far too busy to notice who goes around with whom,' he said. 'Naturally the academics have a lot to say to each other as they are colleagues and they may meet only at the various international conferences. So I'd say it's likely to be an academic. How are you getting on? Shall we be able to leave tomorrow?'

'We're trying to eliminate everyone here as soon as possible,' said Falkner, 'but this new murder complicates the thing. I've got every available detective busy taking statements. I hope most of your members will be able to leave. It's a complication that so many of them come from abroad. Once they've left it won't be easy to get them back.'

When the PC on the door had closed it behind Martin, Charter said, 'My talk with Lord Hellvellyn's sister-in-law brought out this. Matthew Frost took his money out of BCCI in time not to lose too much of it. I don't know how she knows this or how accurate it is.'

'I've got his financial affairs under scrutiny. But it all takes too long. We must establish whether Mrs Wallace and Frost are having a fling. Could you have a word with Ninian Wallace? I'd like to know more about that lady's movements. And by the way she's a big, strong girl. Thin but wiry.'

'I wouldn't rule her out. Where and when do we meet again?'

'Play it by ear. I'm up to my eyes.'

*   *   *

Charter went out into a sudden shower of rain. He found Ninian walking up and down at the edge of the Upper Lake. It was quite a severe summer rainstorm and the water was dimpling wildly under the shower of drops. Ninian's hair looked dark, plastered down on his forehead. Drops ran down his nose and plopped on to the jersey under the open anorak.

Charter turned up the collar of his jacket and buttoned it up as he ran across to join him.

Ninian walked on morosely and Charter fell into step beside him.

'May I ask you a few questions? I'm helping the local police get the picture straight.'

Ninian looked sideways at him and then looked away again. 'Of course,' he said.

'What were you looking for downstairs in the hotel last night?'

Ninian stopped dead then walked on even faster.

'I was looking,' he said furiously, 'for my wife. I woke up to find she wasn't in her bed so naturally after a while I got up and went to look for her.'

'And didn't find her?'

'No I didn't.'

'And when did she return?'

'At three o'clock. She may have left the room before midnight for all I know. Three hours! I made the obvious inference. She'd gone to someone's bed.'

'And had she?'

'She won't say. She hit me across the face when I asked her. She won't say a word to me this morning. It's ludicrous. You'd think I was the guilty one.'

'Can you make a guess at who she was with?'

'What? No. I'm going to file for divorce. If she'd been sorry ... but to hit me in the face! What's got into her?'

'I'd better have a word with her.'

'You can't. She's gone back to London

again.'

'Has she indeed. I may have to go and see her there in that case. What's the address please?'

Ninian scribbled it down.

'Thank you, Mr Wallace. Now it does occur to me that Mr Frost came back to the North of Trent yesterday. His wife wasn't with him. Do you think perhaps it could have been his room your wife went to?'

'Matthew Frost? You've got to be joking. He's a roughneck.'

'I see. And you've no idea? You see it's very important to find out people's movements last night during the hours when Professor Kenworthy might have been killed.'

Ninian looked at him. His eyes narrowed and he frowned.

'I'm sorry,' he said sullenly. 'I can't help you.' He folded his lips obstinately.

'Just one last thing,' said Charter. 'Have you any idea who were Professor Kenworthy's friends in the society?'

'Kenworthy? I don't know that he foregathered with anyone in particular except, during this conference, Bracousse. And in Venice, now that I come to think of it, he and the journalist, Dermot Finn, were always together. They used to get a bit rowdy in the evenings. Martin got quite annoyed with them.'

Charter went straight back to Victoria.

'Mrs Tallent,' he said, 'I've just had to ask

Martin Proctor who were Professor Kenworthy's closest friends in the society. He couldn't help. But Ninian Wallace talks of Finn, the journalist. What would you say?'

'It's no use asking Martin about that sort of thing,' she said. 'He wouldn't notice. But Ninian would.'

'So Kenworthy and Finn were very friendly during the Venice conference but they haven't gone near each other at this one?'

'Now you come to mention it, no. I haven't seen them together this time. They must have quarrelled. They were inseparable in Venice. I remember laughing myself into tears late one night in the gardens at the *pensione* where we stayed to see them both on their knees serenading Rosie Finch both with what Finn calls "the drink taken".'

Charter went back to Ravenshead deep in thought. Had Kenworthy consulted Finn and had Finn talked about Kenworthy's misgivings? Had Kenworthy died for that indiscretion? Finn always would talk in order to tease out another aspect of the same story. Surely Kenworthy knew that?

Falkner was preoccupied. 'Look, John,' he said. 'Why don't you take a look at Lavinia Wallace's statement and check it with her. She's gone back to London? You seem to be a dab hand at getting long stories out of people.'

Charter took the train up to London arriving at the Wallace flat at seven p.m. as he had arranged on the telephone with a reluctant but finally docile Lavinia.

'Sit down,' she said. 'I shan't offer you a drink because you're on duty and the sooner this is over the better I'll be pleased. So let's start.'

'Do you and Mr Frost work on RPS affairs together?'

'Yes.'

'He confides in you?'

She looked at him coldly. 'I don't know what you are suggesting but yes, he does.'

'In the office?'

'And elsewhere.'

'So your relationship with Mr Frost is very close?'

'Very close.'

She looked at him challengingly.

'And does your husband share in this close relationship with Mr Frost?'

'He has nothing to do with it. If what you are leading up to is whether Mr Frost and I are lovers I suggest you ask Mr Frost.'

'I had no intention of going so far so soon,' said Charter, 'though, since you mention it, we do have to investigate the relationships between suspects.'

'Suspects?'

'Yes, Mrs Wallace. Everyone involved in that conference is a suspect until we eliminate them. That's what I'm here for. To eliminate you and your husband.'

'Of course I'm glad to help,' she said mildly.

'Did Mr Frost and the professor meet on his last trip to England in July this year?'

'They met briefly at the Dorset Square for breakfast.'

'Do you know the purpose of the meeting?'

'No purpose. It was a routine meeting on RPS business.'

'Could Mr Frost have been trying to sell something to the professor?'

He was taken aback by her reaction. She turned chalk white and lay back gripping the arms of her chair until her knuckles turned white.

'Are you ill, Mrs Wallace? Shall I get you a glass of water?'

'Yes please.'

He found the kitchen and brought her a glass of water with ice in it.

The ice chinked in the glass as she took it. She put the glass down quickly.

'You haven't answered my question, Mrs Wallace.'

'No. I can't remember. What was it you said?'

'Did Mr Frost plan to sell something to the professor?'

'No, of course he didn't. Mr Frost doesn't sell things to his friends. What could he possibly want to sell? They discussed the plans for the society that's all.'

'Was Mr Frost engaged on some literary

work?'

'He was working on a paper for the society but he's been so busy that he hasn't been able to get on with it.'

'Where did he do this work?'

'At the London Library.'

'Not at Melbourne Hall?'

'He did go there once or twice.'

'And he didn't make what he thought might be an astonishingly important literary find at Melbourne Hall?'

Her teeth chattered on the glass as she picked it up and sipped from it.

'No. I'm sure he would have told me if that had been the case.'

'Did he meet Professor Pomfret at Southwell and exchange this literary find for a large sum of money in Swiss francs?'

'If he did he didn't tell me.' Her eyes were on him, strained and questioning. It was a look of anguish. Then she said, 'Well, I did suspect he had made some sort of discovery.'

'And he badly needed money didn't he?'

'Yes,' she said eagerly, 'he did. He had lost money over the past year.'

'So he might be tempted to do something he considered mildly dishonest?'

'Now that he's so over-extended business-wise who knows what he might do.'

'I see.'

'Well,' she said, with a show of reluctance, 'I don't like to reveal things I've learned through my job but I can see that this is very important. He's a Name.'

'At Lloyds?'

'He's been one for years. Everything was fine until last year. He got into a very bad syndicate. He lost a fortune and the awful thing is that he stands to lose as much again for the next I don't know how many years. I don't know how serious it is. He may be able to cover his losses. He's made a lot of money out of Lloyds in the past. But he may be in serious difficulties.'

'Mrs Wallace, do you want to telephone your husband? As a purely routine exercise we are going to have to search your flat. It's annoying for you but it won't take too long.'

She looked quite calm.

'Just get on with it will you?' she said.

So the money was clearly not hidden in the flat.

CHAPTER TWENTY-FOUR

I see the whole design.

BROWNING

The first thing Falkner said next morning when he and Charter arrived simultaneously at Ravenshead was, 'Lord Ralph Kerr telephoned you last night. Will you call him back now?'

But Lord Ralph had left for London.

'Search of the Wallace flat negative,' said Falkner. 'Did you get anything useful from her?'

'I got an absolute conviction that she is involved. Either she did it alone or with Frost or with someone else. As soon as I mentioned a possible literary find and sale of a manuscript to Professor Pomfret she began to shake and started volunteering damaging information about Frost.'

'So Frost is presumably not the lover she went to at the North of Trent?'

'Wallace said Frost would be a non-starter with his wife and I don't see her initiating any of this. No imagination. Not dynamic.'

'Could Andrew Tierney be the lover?'

'Even less her type I'd have thought.'

'Lavinia would be the best possible accomplice in this game. Through being married to the deputy chairman and being secretary to RPS and to Matthew Frost she knew all the things the hoaxer needed to know. In particular she knew about the recorded messages. It was common knowledge in the society that these messages were played every year at the dinner. But she would actually be organizing the tape recorder. She would probably load the machine herself before it went over to the cloisters. So there'd be no need to switch tapes. She'd simply load the wrong tape and ditch the other. And then she'd make sure the recorder was sitting there in the cloisters for long enough to give a hoaxer the opportunity to switch tapes. She didn't need to wipe off her fingerprints as she was handling the recorder legitimately but I reckon she's clever enough to have wiped all fingerprints off anyway because that's what the hoaxer would do after he'd loaded the tape.'

'Lavinia's clever. As soon as I suggested that she was the only person who could have suppressed the letter of acceptance from Bracousse she pointed out that anyone with their wits about them would have given him another address for his reply.'

'So Lavinia conspired with Kenworthy?'

'I'm beginning to have my doubts about Kenworthy. He had a lot to look forward to. I wonder whether he'd have jeopardized all that. One thing I'm certain of is that he wouldn't have done it as a practical joke on the professor or to pass it off on him as the real thing in order to cheat him.'

'Would Kristeller?'

'I doubt if the killer would have let either of the academics into the secret that they were planning to sell the fake. Or mentioned who they were going to sell it to. Though it's possible both of them might guess. Kenworthy had tremendous prospects and earns from books as well as his salary. Kristeller isn't at all happy with his career prospects and he doesn't write successful books. He has a king-size chip on his shoulder and he might get a great kick out of a hoax on the academic world with a nice fee thrown in for his trouble.'

'Let's say then that it was Kristeller who prepared the text for the forgery. When he heard of the death of Professor Pomfret and the finding of the body in bizarre circumstances in the Slype he guessed this was somehow connected with the faked memoirs, panicked and fled. Either he thought the whole thing would come out and he'd be thought of as accessory to murder or he feared for his own life.'

'And how right he was to fear for his life. Kenworthy may have copped it simply because he was beginning to make some guesses.'

'And the man Kenworthy talked to? Finn?'

'Finn would fit the bill.'

'He went to Venice.'

'Where he met Lavinia Wallace. Have you seen the piece he did on the society? There's a very romantic photograph of Lavinia late at night under a lamp. Supposing he fell for her in London and carried on the affair in Venice?'

'Fell for Lavinia Wallace? She's a terrifying woman.'

'Look at it like this. Lavinia is the icy and upright Clarissa Harlowe and Finn the lustful unscrupulous Lovelace longing to get that pure unsullied body between the sheets.'

'Would he be capable of the careful, long-term planning?'

'I suppose he might be. And there's something perverse in him. He might even enjoy it. Lavinia would do her part with efficiency and discretion and he'd do his with enjoyment and panache. I don't know why we didn't hit on him earlier.

'Hold your horses, John. Facts.'

'Here's one. Finn lied to me about his reason for being here. I got this from Miss Cunningham and it's been at the back of my mind ever since. It was a stupid thing to do because it was totally unnecessary. As a writer on the Romantics why shouldn't he be here? He panicked when I appeared on the scene and tried to distract attention from his close relationship with RPS. He said he was here specifically to interview Hellvellyn and that Hellvellyn had agreed to be interviewed. In fact Hellvellyn never gives interviews and if he did his ladies would put a stop to it. They had made Finn promise that he wouldn't bother the old boy at the conference and they gave him an interview themselves in exchange for his promise.'

'A man without a conscience.'

'A journalist. Finn would be perfectly capable of stripping the body and carting it around. He's highly intelligent and quick as a monkey.'

'Motive?'

'Money? Money for Lavinia perhaps. I

doubt if he could offer her more than Ninian. He probably rents a bachelor flat. That wouldn't do for Lavinia. He might have done it to be able to keep her in the manner to which she'd like to become accustomed.'

'And she would make the approaches to Pomfret.'

'I think so. As secretary to the society she kept tabs on all the academics. She'd be in on all the decisions about who they'd ask to give papers and who'd be contributors to the journal.'

'Embarrassing for her afterwards with Pomfret.'

'Not in the least. The plan must have been to give up her job and the society and to count it all well lost for Finn. I reckon they'd live abroad. And in any case Pomfret comes over only once or twice a year at most.'

'Look, John, call Lord Ralph. He may have evidence on Frost one way or the other.'

The phone rang and Falkner handed it to Charter. It was Lord Ralph Kerr.

'Is that Mr Charter?' he asked. 'I'm sorry I was away from home when you called. I've been trying to get hold of you to make sure you don't make an unfortunate mistake. My archivist tells me that you suspect Matthew Frost of making off with a copy, or part of a copy, of Byron's memoirs which he found among my books here. I'm quite certain that he did nothing of the kind. He couldn't conceivably steal from me. He's a friend of ours. And in any case he's far too knowledgeable to have been under the impression that he could have sold the thing. I suppose it would belong to me. And I imagine John Murray holds the copyright. It might even be held that it belonged to him. All that sort of thing would have to be sorted out. I'm afraid you've got it wrong.'

'I see.'

'And in any case it isn't the memoirs. He took the pages he found to Digby Tenniel Rufford who is knowledgeable about these things and Digby advised him to forget it if he didn't want to make a laughing stock of himself. It was nothing to do with Byron. Matthew brought it back and we fell about laughing. Then he worked it into a paper for some book collectors up at Grasmere, telling the story as a warning to over-enthusiastic book collectors.'

'Can you tell me the date and the venue of the Book Collectors' weekend?'

'The Wordsworth Trust up at Grasmere. I can't remember the date but some time in the early spring.'

'Thank you very much indeed.'

Ringing off, Charter gave the thumbs up to Falkner and called the Wordsworth Trust at Grasmere. He put a young woman up there to work and in a few minutes she was back on the line with the date and a list of participants in

207

the conference.

He turned to Falkner. 'Robert,' he said, 'I think we've got him. Got his name, I mean. Not a scrap of evidence. It'd give the DPP a nervous breakdown. But it's our man. The fair Lavinia's lover, the man who met Lord Hellvellyn at a Book Collectors' weekend and heard Matthew Frost give a paper describing the mistake he'd made when he found some papers at Melbourne Hall which he took for part of a copy of Byron's memoirs. That gave Finn the idea of producing the fake copy of the memoirs and selling it. Lavinia probably told him who would be in the market for it. Then he thought up the series of hoaxes to persuade the professor that the theft of the faked memoirs was just another hoax. Lavinia would give him all the information he needed for arranging the hoaxes. I reckon he enjoyed every minute of it until he struck out at Pomfret in a panic and killed him. Look, I'll go and see Victoria Tallent right away and see if there's any evidence of a liaison between Finn and Lavinia.'

'I'm seeing them all in the Orangery in half an hour so get on with it. I'm going to have to let them go but first I'm going to have a brainstorming session and find out if anyone has any evidence on Pomfret's movements at Southwell.'

Charter found Victoria gathering herself together for the slow walk over to the

Orangery.

'Come on then, dear,' she said, 'you walk me over and we'll have a little talk on the way.'

'Do you remember telling me that you saw Ninian Wallace walking about in the middle of the night and you hoped he wasn't visiting someone?'

'Yes I do.'

'Well we think it wasn't Ninian but his wife who was visiting and it's rather important that we should find out who.'

'Lavinia? Oh dear, poor Ninian.'

'Do you think she might possibly have been running an affair with Dermot Finn which must have been going on for over a year?'

'I did see them together once or twice in Venice but I didn't think anything of it because he was interviewing a lot of us for his article. I have noticed that the Wallaces haven't been getting on well. They've always bickered but lately she has been much worse.'

He left Victoria in the Orangery which was already full of slightly nervous members and paced up and down the cloisters thinking about Finn. As yet there wasn't any evidence fit to take to the DPP though there might well be some when all the statements about times and who saw who doing what, where, on the evening of the dinner, had been assessed and fed into the computer. But that result would be complicated by the people who couldn't remember times and by anyone who had lied.

Finn would have lied and so would Lavinia.

Finn had been very clever. He had burned the faked manuscript as well as the bloodstained clothes, his own as well as the professor's. He had probably stripped naked in the dark before hitting Kenworthy over the head and might well have slipped into the stewpond beside the body to wash off any evidence before dressing again. The tape recorder had been handled only by Lavinia who was the legitimate user of it. The cassette tape had vanished for the time being into thin air and so had a fortune in Swiss francs. Eventually evidence might be found in Italy from the place where he bought explosives to use in the boat incident or the accomplice he hired to do it for him. But it was all taking too long. The whole case was insubstantial in the extreme though he was sure that Falkner too believed that Finn was their man.

CHAPTER TWENTY-FIVE

—how is truth to be got at?
We don't arrive at it by standing on one
leg.

BYRON

Two good men had been killed and Finn evidently found that a price worth paying for the safety of his own skin. He must be stopped. He could think of only one way to stop him.

He walked back to the crypt and met Finn coming in through the entrance.

'Finn,' he said, 'I want a word.'

Finn smiled easily. 'I'm supposed to be going to listen to your Chief Super in the Orangery,' he said.

Charter began to walk up and down the stone-vaulted under-croft past the tombs of Little Sir John of the Great Beard and his son and grandson. Finn fell in beside him, his hands in his pockets.

'Finn,' said Charter, 'we're stumped. This man has been altogether too clever for us. We've got to let all these people go home but we've not a shred of evidence and not a hope of making an arrest before they take off. There's only one chance.' He walked on in silence.

After a while Finn said, 'One chance?'

'Lavinia Wallace.'

'Lavinia?' His voice was carefully quiet and even.

'I'm coming to the conclusion that Lavinia is in this. What do you think? I need something more to go on before I take it to my colleagues. I think she helped someone make the plan to steal the manuscript back from Professor Pomfret.'

'Steal a manuscript? What manuscript?'

'That's what all this has been about. A plan to defraud Professor Pomfret using the series

211

of hoaxes as a smoke screen. Professor Pomfret walked out of his bathroom at the wrong moment and the thief, who had thought he was safely at the reception with the rest of the party, panicked and hit out at him. I think it was by mistake that he killed him.'

'Oh,' said Finn in a conversational tone, 'so that's what it was all about. Surely a respectable woman like Lavinia Wallace couldn't have had anything to do with it?'

'You'd think not. But she isn't happy with her husband and I think someone involved her in a nasty piece of fraud which ended up with two murders. Kenworthy's was brutal murder but a woman could have done it. He was taken by surprise. And he was killed near the stewpond alone in the dark. It was easy to push his body in. You must have found the other one much more difficult and risky.'

Finn turned and was running up the South Staircase like a hare, Charter after him in a flash. As he ran into the Great Hall Finn was fiddling with his belt and he produced a mobile telephone. Charter came up with him and held out his hand for the telephone.

'Come on, Finn,' he said. 'This won't do any good.'

Finn put out a hand to ward him off and backed away.

'Lavinia,' he said into the receiver, 'are you there Lavinia?' Then he looked up at Charter. 'You would pluck out the heart of my mystery,' he said before Charter took the phone and raised it to his ear.

'Mrs Wallace,' he said urgently, 'Mrs Wallace. Listen to me. Mr Finn and I are coming to see you to work out mitigating circumstances. It's going to be all right.'

There was no reply.

Charter turned on Finn. 'Get me her number,' he said. 'Come on, Finn. Do you want her to take an overdose?'

'Let's talk,' said Finn. He fastened the phone into the case on his belt and walked quickly away beside the rope that cordoned off a corridor for visitors.

Charter walked after him. 'Look,' he said, 'you know it's all up. I've got to give all this to Falkner. But I'll do what I can for both of you.'

'Nothing could mitigate it for her. She's finished, but do tell me about the mitigating circumstances.' He turned and came to meet Charter with a wide smile. Then he gave him a great shove that sent him reeling back and was over the rope in a flash and, seizing a heavy candlestick that stood on a refectory table, rushed at Charter raising it above his head. As Charter swung round and put up an arm to protect himself Finn brought the candlestick down, aiming at his head, his face distorted by the effort and his own stark terror. The candlestick bruised and almost broke Charter's arm and caught him a glancing blow on the head as he ducked away. Blood spurted

213

over Finn and blinded Charter. He kicked Finn in the groin and, as he doubled up, ran out of the Great Hall and along the gallery. Finn still held the candlestick and Charter chose to seek the high ground by making for the spiral staircase up to the Oratory and Byron's bedroom. There, two or three steps above Finn, and the murderous candlestick would lose its power. Much better than sprinting down the South Staircase with Finn above him. By the time he reached the stairway and leaped up the first three steps, Finn was already at the bottom.

'Put that thing down,' said Charter. 'You can't hit me with it from there. Look, you know as well as I do that if you'd killed me with it just then you wouldn't have stood a chance.'

'You're the only one who knows,' said Finn.

'Don't be so naive. Do you think Falkner doesn't know all I know and more? We've worked all this out together. All we need is evidence and by hitting me with that thing you've given us something like it. They're already searching the Wallaces' flat. Do you really think she won't lead them to you? She broke at the first mention of the sale of a literary discovery. The circumstantial evidence alone is almost conclusive. Now they'll get the rest. It's only a question of time. You can't beat the computers and the lab. And you can't hope to get to the money. They've been following all of you wherever you go.'

'You see,' Finn said, 'I couldn't go to prison.' He let the candlestick drop to the floor and was fishing in his pockets. And now he drew out a Swiss army knife and snapped it open.

Charter looked at him hard. 'Don't use it, Finn,' he said.

'It's not for you,' said Finn in a conversational tone. Calmly he drew the blade across his left wrist and smiled up at Charter.

'I "smote him thus",' he said.

Charter jumped down and closed with him so that both of them fell to the floor. He had Finn by the hand that held the knife and jerked it so that the knife shot away along the gallery. Finn kicked him hard on the chin as he broke away and flung himself after the knife, picked it up and was away at the other end of the gallery holding the blade to his throat as Charter came after him, reeling and stumbling.

'Stop,' he said, 'or I'll do it this way.'

Charter stopped and Finn brought his right wrist across to the knife he was still holding in his left hand. Sweat stood out on his forehead as he drew the wrist across the blade and made another deep cut. Then he went chalk white and sat down on the floor. 'It takes a little time,' he said and closed his eyes.

Charter bent down to take the knife and the telephone. When Finn heard who he was speaking to and what he said he opened his eyes and said furiously, 'Leave her alone.'

215

Pools of blood were growing on the floor as it slowly seeped out of him.

Charter finished calling his colleagues on the phone and shouted for help.

The custodian came running and found him pressing pads made from the shirt he had stripped off, to each of Finn's wrists. Under instruction from Charter he tore his own shirt into strips and was binding up the bandages when several PCs arrived. The keepers of the art collection came and leaned over Finn and offered tea. He opened his eyes and smiled and said, 'Oh lovely.' He was still smiling as they carried him away.

Charter noticed the custodian and the keepers looking at him in some dismay and went off to seek his room at the North of Trent to clean himself up. In the crypt he met Falkner who was white with rage.

'I know, I know,' said Charter. 'Come over when you've time and say it all. But we've got him.'

'We've got evidence on Lavinia Wallace and we might by now have had something on Finn too, without all this carnage.'

'It looks much worse than it is. What have you got?'

'It's not all that much as she didn't recognize her, but Daisy Masters went from the bar at the Saracen's Head, where you saw her with Andrew Tierney at lunchtime on Saturday, to Southwell Minster. She wanted to buy a

216

religious art book for her mother's birthday from the bookstall. And there she saw Professor Pomfret on his knees but not at prayer. He was chatting to a tall, dark-haired woman who came into the church carrying a parcel and made a bee-line for the professor, whom Daisy had met at the hotel. The woman was wearing dark glasses and a panama hat pulled well down over her eyes.'

'The fair Lavinia! In disguise!'

'You'd better see a doctor. We'll talk later.'

Charter omitted to see a doctor but spent the next hour once he had cleaned up his wound, lying on his bed feeling rather ill but fairly self-satisfied.

Falkner came up to see him there an hour later in a much more cheerful mood.

'He told my sergeant where he hid the money,' he said. 'Very clever. Like Charles the Second. In a tree. A PC went up and found it in a plastic bag hanging high up in the branches of a chestnut tree where the leaves hang so thickly that there wasn't a chance of anyone seeing it until autumn thins the leaves. I must say the man had a very busy night that Saturday: making bonfires, sending extra copy to his paper, climbing trees to hide the loot and knocking out distinguished detective officers. I hope you're feeling better.'

'Beginning to.' Charter felt the bruise on his chin.

'In that case.' Falkner produced a bottle of

champagne. 'This stuff is supposed to be good for nursing mothers so I doubt if it will do you any harm.'

*   *   *

The Nottinghamshire Police prepared to go back to Sherwood Lodge. Charter gave a final glance at Corinna who was standing between Matthew and Andrew on the steps of the hotel, frowning. She met his eyes and slipped a hand in to the arms of her father and her husband.

'Come on,' she said, and they turned away, united in their distaste for him and of what he had suspected them.

Chief Superintendent Falkner came over to shake him warmly by the hand.

'We'd never have done it so quickly without you,' he said.

'We did it together,' said Charter. 'Not everyone would have given me so much rope.'

'We'll meet and talk it over one day.'

'One day. Yes.'

Falkner got into his car and was driven away.

The last of the police cars drove off past the North of Trent and disappeared round the bend in the drive.

Charter dug his hands into his pockets and trudged off towards the car-park, his eyes on the toes of his brogues.

After a while a pair of leather sandals moved

up beside them stepping lightly along at his side and Sophie put an arm through his. They walked together to the car-park in companionable silence.

'I tell you what,' said Sophie as they reached her hatchback. 'Are you heading for home?'

'Yes.'

'Not going straight to Ireland?'

'No, not today.'

'Then let's meet at the Bridge Inn half-way and have lunch together. Shall we?'

He put an arm round her and held her tight for a moment.

'Yes, Sophie,' he said. 'Let's do that.'

We hope you have enjoyed this Large Print book. Other Chivers Press or Thorndike Press Large Print books are available at your library or directly from the publishers. For more information about current and forthcoming titles, please call or write, without obligation, to:

Chivers Press Limited
Windsor Bridge Road
Bath BA2 3AX
England
Tel. (01225) 335336

OR

Thorndike Press
P.O. Box 159
Thorndike, Maine 04986
USA
Tel. (800) 223–6121 (U.S. & Canada)
In Maine call collect: (207) 948–2962

All our Large Print titles are designed for easy reading, and all our books are made to last.